Colm Michael O'Driscoll

NAG
need a god

europe books

www.europebooks.co.uk | info@europebooks.co.uk

ISBN 9791220139571
First edition: April 2023

NAG
need a god

Chapter 1

So, It Is! Amen!!

It's a fly, by a rock pool.

"Haven't seen you in years!!" Clem says.

"Well… not you, but your grandfather." Clem starts the calculation in his head.

'About fifteen years since I've seen one of you, so it's…' He without calculating much further accepts it is indeed many generations on.

It is March, mid-morning, mild but a little sting of winter lingers. He considers himself and slowly lifts his view to the cliffs.

"So that's how you see me!! I'm the fly!

"You've seen my parents and grandparents!!!... And all before me."

Clem looks to the sky. The moon is in the right quarter.

"And you, you have seen the cliffs move like Olympic athletes… and us," his voice fades "crawl from the sea." It's the death of heaven. He sees it now.

Clem smiled oddly, he'd struck upon something that had engulfed him of relief and fear. Inside, he didn't want to be right on this but it was time to start facing facts. It is a search that he alone, without assistance, decided to embark upon. He felt closer to the essence of the universe. Had it eaten and fascinated him all this time?

"So what force is there? That relates to the moon as it does the cliffs, to humans as to the fly?"

"The stars!" As he spoke it, he thought, *'just another step'*. "Big Bang! Or God?"

He paused on that thought and instead moved to the thought of humanity. He knows we have crawled from the sea. This is indisputable now.

"Why have children stillborn?" he asks.

"Why have a baby die after a second, ten seconds, a minute, twenty minutes, a day, a week." Clem starts to walk along the beach, removing himself physically so his mind may follow, for he is not entirely comfortable with the depth to which this subject could lead.

"Like roadkill, like the carcass of rabbits, crows, cats." He saw a cat once, the silhouette of one, in the glare of his headlights kicking its legs and feet skyward, exhaustive last struggle of life as he drove a secondary country road one night.

"Is that all we are?" he thinks of the food animals become that pass on into the eco chain. He realises we are part of the whole system whether integral or not, he remains unsure, "but we are of it!"

Clem ponders some more, he is now heading away from the beach towards his car. *'What of the first time we as humans see an animal? That experience stays with us. It is carried with us, through our life.'* He continues, *'so we carry experiences with us and pass them on to others. Good, bad, brilliant, mundane.'*

Clem leans against his taxi. "The pain, the joy. Who, what inflicts or impresses us? Everything that has gone before," he answers. "Everything that has ever happened in the universe!!...My first memory?" he ponders. Clem looks quickly around again, enters the car and drives home. It is 2010.

Everything has changed. He's still gambling, if only he could save two thousand euros. He'd put it into a stock account and build from there. He just couldn't stop gambling. He was running away, hiding always hiding.

Why did he keep going? He'd got a loan for his own taxi, no bills with a free run of a relatively big house but he still couldn't stop gambling. It was the draw, the comfort, the ability to hide away from the world outside. He hated it now though. He worked hard but constantly gambled it away. Was this his existence? To go earn, pay some bills and gamble? Surely not? Surely not now? His friends were moving on, getting girlfriends, marrying, having babies, buying houses. He'd seen enough as a child to believe this was not necessarily the only way.

It wasn't always glory and light and somewhere behind many a four walled house resided a lot of pain. He'd rather be something else but he was pushing on, wasn't this the thing to do though?

Yes, but not for him, not now anyway, not yet. *'But when? Maybe never.'* He'd seen his parents ending up in dead-end existences. Glossed over by time and false memories. But pain had existed, lots of it. Clem wanted glory, comfort, sweetness. He really didn't know what he wanted. As imperfect as his father was, his mother, a lovely woman, was no saint either. Whether they were loyal to each other sexually or not, he presumed so, but assumed nothing, for if their loyalty to each other led to this, then what was the point.

Clem had to call to mum, it was Saturday, the day he brought her for a spin. Saturdays had drawn tiresome. Mother was heading back toward dementia, old age and poor health.

The process began. "Will we be back for tea?" Up to two hundred questions in over an hour. The stop in the carpark. The walk to the shop. Tea, loads of milk no sugar. Latte. A cream doughnut. The return to the car. Fast eating, fast drinking, questions coming through the bubbles, coughing. Spillage. Cleaning, Clem wasn't fussed on that. It happens. It was a little annoying. No answer he gave ever enough. It had driven his father crazy. It was easy to see why. It hurt, it frustrated. It was a case of being there, wanting to be there was not the purpose. She suffered the most. Clem knew that, they all knew that. In the midst of all the questions she was still there, conscience. *'Seeing oneself frustratingly suffer a mental form of incontinence, that must be a really really strange thing to witness.'* He could understand.

Clem had done it. Did it all the time. That point where he'd do or say something that was done by the time he tried to stop but Clem still had brakes. He could still pull it, recognise it, steer it. This control was gone from his mother.

Saturday duty was done, he needed a rest. Away. A few hours in bed, an hour in front of the television.

It was just a mess. And Clem's life without a mess was as normal as it was with one. A million euros and he'd be out of there. Everything would be so different. Somewhere, someday down the line he'd get there but it hadn't happened yet, already all these years on. Still gambling, still hoping, still losing, inherently self-destructive. He promised himself so many times as he left the casino, *'this will be the last time ... I promise!'*

He pulled at every piece of symbolism going. It was likely he'd be there again tomorrow or in two days or three. The hours crept by, turned to days, months, years. He was heading towards forty now. Too old for a lot of things, still time if he got his act together. He'd run away so many times.

The second time when he was eighteen, he was staying in the college suburbs. He'd turned into a petty thief and got rumbled. Gambled it all. He returned home. Got his bicycle the following morning and traded it in for enough money to get a ticket to London. Walked fifty miles that day, hungry with barely enough to rattle in his pockets, making it to his Aunt's house and waited a few days for his brother to collect him. He'd survived. Situations would happen, had happened, in his family life, getting himself into needless bother but he would survive.

Between thirty and forty he settled a bit. No relationships. They were still wishy-washy affairs, hypothetical as much as real. He formed two great friendships though. They would be a great help and bring some semblance of normality to his life. Clem was a misfit of sorts, fundamentally happy with life but having to dust himself down more regularly than most, finding the will to get up and fight again, that was getting harder.

It was sticking out, starting to. What a lot of people said. Clem needed to get two tyres changed. The guy was in the cabin of the workshop. Clem walked through and knocked.

"What can I do for you?" the worker asked.

"Two tyres, front right and boot!" Clem suggested.

It was cold. A sharp wind blew along the quiet street. The worker was well covered in clothes. His runners, nondescript health issue, pushed against the pedal to start the turning wheel. Clem didn't ask himself how many times those dirty oily runners pushed that pedal, he stopped in the flow of thought, he didn't need to know. Clem waited, not too long, but waited. He'd been there last month and waited then too.

"What is it?" Clem asked, "the tyres! They're gone I'd say," he continued.

Hoping it was only a puncture but if it was a tyre, then it was a tyre. He just really wanted it to be over. To be away. It didn't hold him, but for a second, the trainers did.

"I'll have a look at them for ya."

"Ta!" Clem said.

A man, in a pick-up, just taking off was reaching to light a cigarette "You should…" he paused in mid-stream, "you're right too." It was still cold. The wind.

"Are ye busy?"

"Nah!" Clem hadn't thought much about the answer but it was the easiest one, the one that had least follow on.

"Ye?" he asked.

"Nah, dead." The worker was as reluctant as Clem about a conversation. A local old guy, Clem recognised his face, something seemingly strange or wrong with him passed by, he'd been involved in a football team or a small bookie, he was stretching to say something, looking, waiting for something from Clem. Two birds caught his attention in the sky. Clem managed an acknowledgement of the man, with his head. He turned away, that was enough.

"The boss is a bollocks… always moaning when it's quiet," the worker said.

"I know, they're always the same," Clem agreed. The wind still stinging.

"The winter's a bitch here I'd say," Clem claimed.

The worker gave him an affirming look.

"Do you work days or nights?" the worker asked, the questions still basic.

"Nights," Clem answered.

“Couldn’t do those days? Hanging around, traffic!” the worker replied. Clem could see he was saying it from experience, he knew about waiting, just waiting.

“As bad and all as I am now, I’d go completely crazy if I did days,” Clem offered.

“Yesterday was busy but the rest of the days are…” the worker needed to say no more. They knew. It ended up being only two punctures. It was good to be in the warmth of the car, driving.

Conversations, all the conversations. People gave themselves up in conversations. Clem had had too many of them. The conversation with that worker was fine. He knew, he knew Clem knew. There wasn’t the need for extra words. It wasn’t their thing. Clem needed the tyres repaired, the worker needed to work his hours.

Chapter 2

Why Are We Here?

Clem has been driving a taxi for nine years. He's forty years old now and counting down the days until he leaves Ireland and heads for Spain. Two hundred and sixty-four days. There's a girl, *'there's always a girl.'* They met once, only once, two and a half years ago in Zaragoza. Their friendship, as modern ones sometimes do, grew over the internet.

Both are complex, seem quite open but are terribly shy, and extremely stubborn. He has decided after a few aborted attempts to make a permanent move. Well, permanent enough to give it a chance anyway. Mariella, could well be making a fool of him or visa verse.

It was November now, 2011. The economy in Ireland was grim. It had been late June when Clem set his 'plan' in place. On a wet summer's evening he went to work. At four thirty in the evening. Hungover, relative broke, both metaphorically and literally running from the bookies, this time saying nothing, knowing. He did not want to live this life anymore. The carpets, the lights, the screens, the sounds, the buzz. He wasn't in here.

Clem wasn't too dismayed about what he was. He seemed okay knowing he could have done more aesthetically but that would be just cheap recognition for toeing a line he didn't believe in. He'd toe the line to some degree, caring for his mother, showing up for things, understanding people. He'd done donkey work and received plaudits for it but that rarely put extra on a kitchen table. Reward was reward. Inside himself there was an issue to deal with that no money, love or praise could answer. That if he could find it, it would be the greatest reward of all.

What did he know? About what? About anything? Too vague! About himself?

He's good at messing up, messing up his life?

According to who? The general consensus, what does that mean? Hmmm...

It was Thursday in June, he just turned on the cab radio. The base was working. It took him a little while to push himself. The base operator was busy. "Car six!!" he checked in for work. "Clem? At this time?" the operator called back. From then he just started working, he worked the weekend, twelve hours each day. He worked Monday, Tuesday, big shifts, big hours. Whatever zone he was in, he didn't want to be disturbed. There was the odd call from inside his mind, *'take a break'*, *'an hour'*, *'you deserve it!'* He was calm, ignored himself.

He worked hard and within two weeks he'd around fifteen hundred euros. Picked the seventh of August 2012 as a confirmed date for departure. He told everyone and anyone, whether they wanted to listen or not, he knew he was doing it to brainwash himself.

On July twenty-seventh, he walked away from the bookies for the last time. "One year, just give it one good year!" He worked well until the end of August and was above three thousand euros. He had opened an investment account. Clem had completed a stock market course two years previous, he acknowledged the importance of money for this period, this was everything that he was. As that part inside of him, fought with the part of him that was pushing him on. Clem was determined to use every means possibly to get the task done.

Mariella and his online relationship was hitting another rocky patch. They had a blazing row which ended in him deleting her in late September… She was about to set him up. He'd begged for a day and half but when she was ruthless, she was ruthless. Clem continued with his plan. He wanted her in his ideal world but he also knew he really wanted out of this one. It was his 'leap of faith'. She'd be a prize at the end of this but he was also using it to drive himself. He wanted to leave with about forty thousand euros. He'd love to have sixty thousand, but he'd accept twenty thousand as a minimum… he'd still go with ten.

September, October and Clem started running out of steam. Twelve-hour shifts started turning into ten, to eight, to six or seven… enough to keep him going, without adding to or detracting from his lump sum which stood at six thousand. He'd lost twelve hundred in the stock market, he'd leave those shares alone and go long.

Clem, had been drifting back to the question. It was a way to stop thinking of Mariella. *'You think of that! ...instead of distracting me from getting money together,'* he'd scold himself. It would be good to be rid of as much emotional baggage when he boarded that plane. He'd deal with it now! For the duration, as best he could. He had to keep going.

'My first memory?' he asked himself. *'My first memory, that is still with me, it's a poor one, I remember falling out of a cot. And then, my grandparents in dark clothes, climbing to the landing of the stairs, before coming to my side.'*

His mother told him stories of how he sat on his grandfather's knee and wouldn't say a word. Clem didn't remember it now but could remember remembering a gold and red lid of a small tea-chest. *'I managed to get my hands on it once, I didn't like the contents. It was better with the lid on. I don't think I liked my grandparents either.'* Clem paused thinking if he had to go on with it.

'I remember baby food, then it was changed for something gruesome. Why this, instead of the other stuff? …the beginning of what's good for you!'

He again ventured back into his memory. One morning the kitchen was busy but not loud. There were figures, people. Other people existed. He'd a new coat. Dark blue with a red ladybird pattern. Clem stayed in the corner of the kitchen. Out of the way but in the way of the door that led to the side drive. The figures left one by one and as the door swung back to close, the space in the kitchen grew, until the door remained closed. Absence. Only that person in the chair between the fridge and the table remained. She was his favourite thing in the world. She would pick him up and swing him wildly before chewing into his cheek. It was wonderful.

Between the ages of four and seven, memories become a little more lucid. By the time he was seven, he had learnt to hate! He learnt to steal.

A neighbour's friend worked in the post office and dropped Clem and Peter twenty yards from the school gate every morning. They waited through all weathers for the fat grey man, Mr. Andersson, to open the gate. They were always the first there. He was liked by most kids, Clem was indifferent. They played in the yard until it was time for assembly. The nuns would bring them to the class. When the coldest part of winter arrived, they skipped assembly and went straight to the classroom. Older neighbourhood children, Tim and Brian started coming too, they had a bigger school nearby.

Biscuits. The sister had a box of biscuits that she would hand out as a reward for good behaviour. Iced caramel biscuits. Clem loved those biscuits. Every morning, the box became more and more tempting. He can't remember precisely the moment they took the first biscuits but as the days went on they took more and more. One day, as they were gathered around the box, the door behind them opened. A strange feeling entered his entire body. Not a good one.

His pockets were stuffed to the brim and only crumbs remained. Crumbs to feed the rest of the class. The rest of the winter was cold in the yard.

The next memory of school was being berated by his mother after walking triumphantly, the one-and-a-half mile home on his own. Not only was it irresponsible but he never told his sister, who up until that point had collected him. It wasn't that he forgot her, he was fed up of waiting, always waiting, so to put an end to this situation he'd resolved to take matters into his own hands. He was promptly ordered to walk back to the school and find her. A week or so later, Clem was allowed walk home on his own.

December now. The effects of the economy were kicking in harder than ever and society never seemed more united in its alienation. The stories of how bad things were, were not entertained in Clem's taxi. Straight to the point, generally.

Clem became a little non plussed about the whole idea. 'Looking for what?' He quickly realised that 'shit happens'. He was really trying to find out stuff about himself, before he got to that day.

Yeah, his father could be an over-the-top at times, seldom, a big violent prick. He'd been getting it in the ear from Kate now on her last three visits. Or was it forever? "He's dead." Clem had trouble for a while after his death. His father was still giving out to him in dreams.

He berated him in those dreams *'Aren't you dead?'* when his father would give out. Clem had summoned the courage to tell him *'Fuck off,'* a few times during those dreams. The thing is Clem had told him in real life too. Were dreams meant to be a place where you said 'I love you'? *'Movie crock.'*

Clem had been like that during the latter stages of his death. One of his regrets was not slipping him more cigarettes on his death bed. His father seemed to be okay with dying more than the rest of them. "It mustn't be that bad, with all those drugs." Clem would prefer to go that way. A year to say goodbye, 'high' on everything. Companionship, which was strange because his father liked time on his own. Was there a bit of his father thinking, *'oh just let me go'*, *'that's enough'*? He died magnificently if there is such a thing.

He'd been a bitch of a patient. A quadruple bypass ten years earlier, ordered not to smoke. Too old, too set in his ways, too independent. It was the spirit of the working class. "I'll do your work, give me my money and don't tell me what to do." If he could only stop telling people what to do, or how to do it himself… "We're all at that!" Clem interjected.

But Clem was Clem, and his father asked what Kate asked, what a lot of people thought. "You're twenty now, what are you going to do with your life? You're twenty-five now what are you going to do with your life? You're thirty now, what are you going do with your life?"

"Don't ya think I'd like to know!" Clem would answer. That vexed him so much. The buffer between any line of crap, any lie, any scheme, to avoid hearing those questions. It was always a kangaroo court, otherwise why were those questions being asked. It was really saying 'fit in', 'don't be weird,' definitely elements of concern, Clem was on his way to a whole lot of sorrow if he didn't stop his ways. It was the most certain thing!

Clem buried it deep. Put it away so deep that those echoes would never come back to him. It might be construed as bottling it up but Clem was happy with the persona he'd developed over the years. Yeah, he was a capitalist now but that was temporary, that was to just get money, to get the hell away from here. He'd drop that cloak in Spain and become himself again.

The problem was Kate with her constant bitching and harping on about the past was ruining Clem's already fulfilled closer on the subject of father. He had huge problems with Kate. She had problems with their father, Clem had. But his problems were as equal if not higher with Kate, personally and with what she represented. Her mantra was mind numbing. Clem came from a family of mantras.

They agreed that the nurture wasn't great. In arguments with Kate he'd argue that it was better to come from a "dysfunctional family," as she'd go on about it so often. "If you came from a perfectly functioning, normal, cradle-to-grave family, you'd be boring!! An endless bore!! The madness one must admit is rather entertaining, enlightening, educational. Yes, there were times it was horrible. But look around you," he suggested, gesticulating around the estate "are they happy? ...That must be the most boring way to live a life ever, drab, dull, dreary, 'Welcome to Stepford!' way to exist of them all!!"

Kate would agree, and then rant off continuing to agree at first before going through a plethora of arguments, calling the whole world 'dumb' before finding herself back at 'why her?'

'Why me?' Clem would think.

Clem had never taken a cold rational look at himself. *'Who's rational?' 'What system? What ideology?'* but he was doing it, taking the modern twenty-first century view of himself as an individual, as a being, as a person. He already knew he was a 'fuck-up,' in that regard but he'd find a conclusion and then challenge that ideology.

Clem and his friends caught frogs. He was remembering again. It was a thing, they just did it. Clem wanted to do it too. They were about eleven or twelve. Clem had been taught how to steal. He became good at it. He was able to slip a glass litre of lemonade down inside the wellington boot in his plastic bag and fill the sides with chocolate biscuits. He was good at catching frogs. He didn't care as much about frogs after that. He didn't like what happened to them in the hands of the boys, but he was good at catching them.

He caught them and chucked them in the box. He was good with bees and butterflies, really good with butterflies but really good at stealing. He'd the knack!

For whatever period, be it six months or two years he was able to whip anything from the store. He didn't like it but he got admiration. Then, one day he got caught, nearly shit his pants and stopped. Why did he go further? Why again did he have to wait until he was caught? Caught by the same person who'd caught him at the biscuits.

He was deathly over the consequences, not the wooden spoon that would be meted out to him but of being bold, being bad in his mother's eyes. She never found out. In one of the lighter moments of the Saturday spins, she spontaneously burst into laughter. On further explanation she'd spotted the bookstore where she hocked her schoolbooks back in the day.

Clem played pitch and putt in the summers. He was okay, but everything was such a deadly competition to him. To be the best. He'd played more often than anyone, and instead of learning the correct techniques, would persist with his own methodology. He would cheat. He would cheat with younger kids. Have them stand near the hole and let it bounce off their shoe if it wasn't going in on its own. Often he'd start again after three holes or two holes because he didn't get the start he wanted. Eventually he would surrender to the guilt.

"So I was a weird child!" Clem interjected, thinking *'where's the crime?'* It took to him that he wasn't always as innocent as he perceived himself to be. He got in trouble? What's the measure? There was no great comfort or pleasure in what Clem was doing.

Clem got better, no cheating, he got to hole thirteen holding a 'hot' score. Hole fifteen holding a hot score. It was more than dribbling through to Clem that as an adult he'd been up to something similar recently enough, accompanied by a Kate cliché in the back of his mind "If you don't learn from history…", "Ah piss off, Kate!"

The memory evaporated. He can't remember a significant roar! But he'd won a provincial chess championship as a child, on his own and in teams, a bit of inner happiness about that. *'But there was no roar there either!!'* He argues.

Echoes came back in his head, *'you never won a school championship'*, tournaments, yes, championship, no, was that a thing to be regretful about? Was it a symptom? He hadn't thought about it for years. With the open field of a provincial championship was he able to be a bit more inconspicuous as opposed the closer environment of the few, up close and personal? Clem wanted to brush it off but wanted to face it too. A Leonard Cohen song, *Bird on the wire,* rang through his mind.

There had been two events in his life, both while driving the taxi, where he had to deal with a situation. Coldly, efficiently, close. Where things depended on him. He'd done it both times with military precision, proficient military precision. He knew that. With all others, the consequences, in his control, were never going to result in death or life. Was it the space for choice in all other events that led to particular failures? Or was he being harsh? He scored winning goals in finals, he scored goals when they were needed, only ultimately to fail and sometimes, not often, he played poorly. Isn't that just life? The way it works, no particular reflection on Clem? Wasn't he just ordinary?

"Clem, what are you up to?" he said loudly to himself. "Is this movie crock?" Were those guys better than him, better because he cracked in certain fields of pressure. Is that why he cracked with women, was he a bit claustrophobic? Was he right to be claustrophobic? *'Maybe.'*

So why are we here? With all that has seemed bold, bad, mediocre or good isn't it just a whole lot of ordinary!

'Really, does that matter? Does it matter at all? Does it still hold a great effect on me now? Come on!!!' yeah, you can see the map but is that going to make Clem run out and murder someone or marry someone because everything is better now, because he realised his father didn't hug him enough?

Once a traveller was in his taxi, trying to do better for himself. He got the flesh beaten out of him every day by his father with a big stick. Everyday, that's something to be a bit messed over. And that traveller was messed up over it but learnt from it. Understood in time, that it was wrong what had happened to him and did something about it. Finding for himself what he thought was the best life for him.

Clem didn't have it that bad. It effected him but it was more an education, a curiosity that held him. The moon, the sky, time, the workings of things. Was it his escape? "Talk to a psychiatrist," Kate goes off in his head again, she's coming home for a holiday soon. "He's a psychiatrist, he's got a PHD!!"

Clem has got "and George Bush was the president of the United States" lined up as a rebuttal to an argument they'll have. Kate hates Bush. She's a socialist, Clem thinks only maybe, she insists on it.

And she'll agree again with him, and Clem will add "and how many people will psychiatrists cure?" and she'll agree some more and she'll find her way back to 'PHD', 'University' and 'Me, Me, Me'… Clem knows he's got his own problems with 'Me, Me, Me' and they come out in him as visible to her, as hers to him.

'What other shit is there?'

Clem parks it, the thinking, the rational, goes working. He's not in the mood tonight. The thinking has taken over his work ethic. Mariella's on his mind. Spain's on his mind, his mum is on his mind, she's supposed to be on his mind. 'Me, Me, Me'. It was just a period thing. A thing to do while he's here, waiting. He wonders, consciously accepting he'd ask himself to stop, upon the notion of self. What is he of?

'You're a taxi driver!' Is that all they see? *'I'm a man who drives a taxi. That person in the bar is not a barwoman, she's a woman who works behind a bar. That beggar on the ground is a human who needs money! That policeman is a man who works… okay, bad example… cheap, Clem, cheap.'* He's driving around, giggling a little to himself. Shrugging his shoulders. As if what does the whole of it matter anyway? To who? Who are 'they'? As much as what Clem is to Clem? As close to gods as much as near to nothing, that's what we are really. Like a lot of pieces of grain. From the skies, that's what we look like, pieces of grain. The day, an ever--changing perspective.

Chapter 3

The 'Brick' Analogy

"I'm a writer" Clem finds it harder to stop himself.

"Poems and a philosophy novel," he adds.

"What do you want to do with your life?"

As he worked nights he was glad that most of his customers were drunk or high or depressed.

"Are you busy?" is usually a customer's first question.

This usually followed, "Hiya."

"Where are you off to?"

Some of the more panicky people might direct the order: "Off to town,"

"Could you take me to wherever etc.," and call out every turn as soon as he'd finish coming out of another.

"How's life?" was generally his first question.

"Great, grand! How about you?"

"I don't know…big picture great, small picture boring."

One of Clem's earliest memories was alcohol and stubble. It was one of the few times he got really close to his father. The smell wasn't kind nor the feel smooth. It wasn't comfortable, nothing like the softness of his mother or female relatives but it was love.

His father loved him, didn't get Clem but loved him. "Classy guy, what a classy guy, the classiest guy in all the parish," remembered him proclaiming. What did he see in that? Why did he love him so much and yet his behaviour betray such true feelings?

The debate on his father was open, two siblings adored him, the others saw the negative and positive.

Was this what 'they' wanted? Were 'they' going to persist with it? 'This is what you have to conclude', was he really going to fall into that suck hole? 'My father didn't love me!!' His father loved Clem. He wasn't great with emotions, but he loved him.

Clem sometime in July of 2010, in the middle of gambling, desperately searching for a way out, came upon a theory, as it was developing then, that many factors were outside his control. The consequences of his actions were 'as often finite as they were infinite.' He drove around many places at night but the reality was his ass rarely left the seat. The possibility was high that his body would get into the car again tomorrow and what he'd done the previous day would have had no meaning.

He could drive a long distance and never get out of the car, like cabin crew doing a return flight to a city, are they really there? Is there any real relevance in that?

"I was in Paris, Barcelona, Rome."

'But you were only ever in the airplane!' Clem would think. He'd been like that once, being in places so he could say he was there.

Many of his customers came from hotels, the town where Clem worked was a hub for Hi-tech and Chemical companies. They went to meetings but just stayed in hotels and taxis, how much of being 'I was there!' is there in that. Clem had overnighted on a train through Switzerland. Was he ever in Switzerland? Technically, yes.

His philosophy that July was, 'that we are all just bouncing off each other,' that 'we're tiny individual pods randomly bouncing off each other and though some individuals pop up more than others, like an 'Elvis' or 'Einstein', the rest are just bouncing off each other, almost invisibly. It has an effect and it keeps going around like 'the butterfly effect' or a 'Mexican wave' at a football stadium. But the day after, does the stadium really give a hoot as it stands there looking at the grass?

Clem was in a weary place at this time. He was lost, thought he knew what he wanted but never could make the first steps. Getting out of here was definitely number one. Doing something, like being a writer was high on the agenda. He'd enough lip service paid, to people, to the institutions, the country, the system. The economy was bad. Ireland had taken more hits. The 'sameness' was perpetuating. Overdue on bills, working hard but not hard enough to jump to the next level, getting nowhere. The numbing sense of Déjà Vu about the whole thing.

He liked to look at the moon, the sky, when it was dusk or dawning. He'd headed off to a beach to get away from things. He'd slip outside the taxi circuit when it was 'tipping', he didn't have it in him, it just wasn't quick enough. Still a little too much time to think. Later, one day he would push.

Mariella had been growing on him, it had already been over a year since they met. She was the latest woman in his sights. Something to aim for. He'd always been into symbolism. Searching for poignancy, searching for a reason, a catalyst, enough to start the ball rolling. To take non-stop from start to finish, to see it through.

It was just too long. Five days strong, seven days strong, he'd delude himself that everything was alright and find a way to let whatever he'd built up slip away. Deliberately so at times. Find himself back in a bookies. Self-destructing.

He'd learned a few things. Not to throw every penny away. When bills really needed to be paid, he had something. He slipped at times and could see the threat of the ground opening up underneath waiting to bury him.

He'd begun to heed warnings. He'd enough of going too far. Limbo had been fine in comparison to the nylon blanket and paper cup at the side of a street waiting to engulf him so many years ago.

But Clem had been in a strange place just after the 'it's a fly' incident. He'd been praying. Goodnight prayers with Mum, her praying to 'M.A.', a couple of times for him. Going to church, lighting a candle, 'wanting to stop', 'wanting to get to Mariella,' anything to come down and stop where his life was, 'something to start it, finally, once.' He really didn't believe in God, had questions. He didn't really know about heaven too. Once he went to the graveyard and found himself asking for his father's help. He didn't really believe in it. He knew it was 'a crock', but he'd seen them do it on television and in movies, he knew it was 'a crock'. He thought of the symbolism in it. He thought something would click inside.

It did. It clicked. Pumping petrol on a late summer evening, he stood tall, just stretching. The moon was huge, not white but cream, it was beautiful, the sky was halfway through nighting over. Another shift awaited. He was renting a car right now because he'd let things slip. Two hundred and fifty needless euros out of pocket every week.

Some peaceful wave came over him. It happened through his life, at moments when panic sets in because trouble was looming. It felt like an epiphany, another one. He was calm again, not so het up, a little blasé. He came up with an equation about life. TIME x ENERGY = LIFE!! He was only a bit of energy! However long it took, he would turn logical, hard-working, it was necessary to get his own car back on the road. He would do it, end of.

That's the thing with life. A thousand euros makes such a difference when its middle point is zero. Life for someone five hundred behind every week and someone five hundred ahead is so very different. He'd done it twice in the last few years. He'd blown it deliberately.

He'd nothing to do with it, he was afraid of success, the darkness allured him. Things would go through his mind. The darkness of the step. The jump, something new, something that wouldn't be with him, all this, gone. What character is that? A success? What do you lose? What fight is left? An excuse!

Clem had been reading, YouTubing, learning. He needed to begin somewhere and went to the start. Socrates, Plato, a lecturer in his cab pointed him to Scotus.

No effect can produce itself.

No effect can be produced by just nothing at all.

A circle of causes is impossible.

Therefore, an effect must be produced.

There it was, Clem was in. Life, metaphysics, theology, logic. What do others know? Believe? Think? What circumstances prevailed when Scotus came up with his proof of a god? What politics governed his mindset? Was he defending all gods or the Christian God? If there was a God why did he pick them?

Smoking, drinking coffee at home, curtains closed, the hood over his head it was time to go to work. He braced himself and pushed. Something inside pushed. Launching a boat, a thought happened and he was off. Eyes to the ground as his feet swung in and out of view. Search for car keys, 'yip'. Open door, close door, walk to car, open door. Get in, switch, feet, pedals, lights…drive and away.

It wasn't totally so tonight. The car was amiss and Clem was out. A Sunday lost due to a job he could have had done Friday but he was able to escape the den of the car for a night. He'd thought he should go to an internet café and write but that would come another day.

The Crane Lane was about the best place for someone of Clem's age, disposition and taste. It was mid-November and one of the busiest places was duly somber for the time of year. A D.J. played to an empty floor, generally. Clem skipped a few moves by the side. He watched the few people that were there mingling. It didn't hold much marvel.

The last time he'd been to the club, a problem again with the car and a fight with Mariella, he'd been a complete asshole. Wandering around as ever before but he was quiet that time. He'd upset a Portuguese guy. Nice, friendly, curious guy. Clem injected a few curt, really hard questions. Clem could do that to an audience, individual, it was a trick. Somehow, someway he'd learned to manipulate susceptive minds. He could enhance them or cruelly hurt them, deeply.

Clem was coming up with many theories and analogies. This night, drinking slowly in the bar, he came upon the 'brick analogy' in the field of his own mind, step by step, adding one logical thought to another. He of course knew of Pink Floyd.

'Life is like a brick… well it's about bricks, as an analogy, there are bricks in the 'wall'. The wall being our existence, no… what we've done, as a species to date. When we are younger, we are told and taught how the wall is built. How it got there and we can see what is happening to the wall, good, bad, indifferent, mundane,

brilliant, mediocre, cruel, kind, everything. The wall is an equation. Everything is an equation, it all boils down to math. What is math? Math is in everything. Music, art, nature. The math in nature dominates our world. The math in society tends to reverberate around time and money.

'So the bricks in the wall, through time, including everyone and everything, has put something into the 'wall' or extracted something from it. We, as we are conceived and further born, have already an influence around us. A lot depends on where in the world we are born and hence what specifics of the 'wall' are dominant.

'This changes the brick pattern of our parents, their desires, sometimes for a while, sometimes for the rest of their lives. As we grow up, we are shown how this 'wall', the 'wall of social fabric', is to be maintained. These are laws, rules, taboos, traditions, etc., The human, with our genetic curiosity for development, tends to be distracted, some may desire but never get to try and use for example, a different colour brick or a different shaped brick or a brick of a different composition.

'We are prompted, cajoled, coerced in a general way. Humans are a curious species. Curious as we are complex and stupid as we are simple. So, we have harnessed food, energy and ping pong balls. The 'bricks' are the components of the social fabric, it's already there… in an ever-changing wall. Sometimes though, a particular brick may not be the perfect one, it serves a purpose on a temporary basis. Most bricks are replaced in time anyway.'

For the next week or two he'd ask the question in his taxi.

"If you were asked to bring a brick to a field, what type of brick would you bring?"

Many customers thought he was 'high'. It would take them a bit to figure out he wasn't but was definitely a 'grass head,' many would conclude. Clem smoked a little, once or twice a year. Coffee and cigarettes, he was mostly caffeine and nicotine. The previous year he'd given up alcohol, there had been no need as he'd later discover. He'd already calmed down a lot over the last six or seven years. He drank only every three or four months now. Clem missed it, the socialising that went with it. It might seem he was harping on for former days but Clem was an optimist by nature, those days had been lived and enjoyed, he was looking forward to more but in a different environment.

"If you were asked to bring a brick to a field, what type of brick would you bring?" again he'd ask.

The answers varied very little, very limited. They really hadn't time to think and Clem started realising that those who answered quickest usually hadn't thought about the question much or the deeper meaning of the question.

"What type of brick?" a stoned Kane asked.

It never took too long to figure out that Clem was sort of a 'weirdo' or 'strange but nice,' he'd twenty-five regular customers at this stage and he'd only started giving out his number a year ago. People liked him. He was never threatening and seemed to understand.

"If you were asked to bring a brick to a field, what type of brick would you bring?" he'd ask again.

"I dunno!!" Some bemused faces would look at him.

"I know… I've too much time on my hands!!" he'd answer.

But he got a bit further with others.

He'd have loved to do it as an experiment. An empty field in Spain and everyone from the bar would get on a bus and place their bricks down and together they would construct a wall.

Because Clem was of a different mindset. He imagined the variety of the bricks would be different. Yes, red and grey ones. Obviously, Lego bricks. Round bricks, triangular bricks, mud bricks, wooden bricks, 'perhaps technically a block' but he'd let it go. Now construct a wall. Who'd be pissed off because they hadn't thought of a certain type of brick when they saw someone else turn up with one. "I was thinking that too!" who'd get upset by "what's going on here? This is stupid," and who would say, "what a great idea for a brick, amazing, just amazing."

Clem thought further on. *'If a boss or government or someone in authority made the request how much duller would it be? Or say for example, if 'Banksy' asked would it be straight red, "let him do the magic with it," or would individuals try really hard to become as creative as possible with them.'*

Now the construction of the wall. A thousand-person democracy. When would they all step back and say, "yeah! I like it that way! It's good!" Who'd be nitpicking to the very end.

Clem would have long gone from the field and come back tomorrow to see what they'd accomplished. *'There's going to be a few,'* he thought, *'it's about finding your brick! What you are! Where you want to put it in the wall. Sometimes you get the sweet spot! Sometimes you get the tough spot, sometimes you really don't care an inch about it but with a thousand people deciding, a side or two might have to be chosen in order to solve an argument or discussion in order to prevent a full-blown row breaking out.'*

The best thing about life as opposed to the brick analogy is you don't have to deal with a thousand people in one place, with equal choice, or thoughts on a particular subject, on any given day. The problem is the ones, twos and threes that represent millions.

He waited around town two weeks later, an auto electrician's "about an hour" was turning out to be a day. Clem had quadrupled many a 'ten minutes' in his own line of work, he knew the score. There was a film festival in town. He glanced through the programme, attracted to a couple of 'existence and life' films. He'd have liked to have gone but he felt he had to develop his mind at his own pace.

He was exhausted again but managed to slip up to mother for a visit. He could hear her asking for whatever it was she wanted next as he came down the hall. It saddened him. Her in the bed, waiting for some mercy to come upon her. She didn't have time even to pray. Clem left quickly enough, he didn't have the energy to keep her company. He kissed her on the forehead and left, she was again asking for her pad, repetitively.

Chapter 4

Falling at the First Hurdle and the Second One

Clem's interest in his wall, the wall that surrounded him, was dead. He'd already left for Madrid in his heart. His mind was part there, his body needed to follow soon. It was hurting lots. He felt himself slipping into an old routine, and progress was stagnating. These questions and logical thinking reminded him of a long-gone mind-set that had prevailed at times through his life, he didn't like the memories. In some bedsit somewhere coming up with a system to beat the house. Night after night, he had been a bit of messed up young man.

He couldn't believe his mind was dragging him back. He'd been rid of it. Whatever world he was in now was far better than anything he'd grown up alongside. The dreaming, one day that it would all come right. He still dreamt but he'd been reaching at shorter odds, at things that didn't have as heavy a price to pay. His big fall back on anything he ever did was 'we die anyway!'

Clem went to work, drifted off into thought again and he remembered remembering driving one day. Hearing during the news bulletin of a young boy who died when his coat got tangled in the door of a bus. It really stuck with him. The near misses as he was growing up. The tragedy for the young boy as the light tumbled round and then…

How many moments like that in his life? The moments of panic. Climbing railings with spikes threatening just underneath his neck. Looking away, waiting, perplexed for moments, for the energy to resolve itself inside, to push hard, as hard as he could away, away to safety. Thinking as you wait, something greater awaits you, squirm and scrawl and crawl. The feeling of death, how suddenly it draws near, waiting for you.

The beauty of looking around at things, because, though this time he lives, there will be a time when it's his last look.

Death is not a fascination for Clem. His greatest fear is never having lived. He is aware of it, when it pops up to remind him of its presence.

'What's living?' he thinks. "What's living?" he speaks. He'd laughed and loved so much at times during his life that they were the only things that existed.

He wonders temporarily how the species continues, accepting evolution as the current staple of his continued search. So what are we to do during life? Live the status quo? Tried and tested, relatively successful, too tedious for Clem?

'Honestly, what is in it? How fulfilling can it be? The species has thrived using this method, so our survival has been guaranteed for a many number of generations. Of course with success come pitfalls. Though, through the centuries the human species has been able to recover.'

One day, we may or may not become extinct. The likelihood is yes but many generations on. *'Who knows?'* Clem guesses the Cold War was the closest we have come. We've had catastrophes before, the plague and world wars but with the capacity for destruction, if to be believed, at the hands of the U.S. and Soviet Union we would have been destroyed.

He remembers being scared by the talk in the school yard. How his classmates yielded so much information.

There were missiles set on every city in western Europe. Clem's town was on the map too. It was only a matter of time. It petrified him, for a while. That's the thing about life. The factors that determine it are as controllable as they are not, there are too many individuals. Clem feels that's where God and then religion come in.

Money always followed, that in itself had an ideology of its own. As unfair a system as it is, it's probably the system that has served the species best until now. It is only a communiqué.

It's a measure, though through luck of the individual parents to breed. 'I was a strong sperm… I made that egg mine. Nine months later…I was born. 1971. The math, the equations in this one feat are phenomenal!!' The years and years of events that have preceded it to make this happen are remarkable, miraculous. Seven billion of those miracles?

Clem had been driving the taxi for thirty days straight now, he's letting everything go with the car, putting the least amount of money into it. Six and a half months left of roadworthiness, he was lucky to pass the last time. Three days before its expiry date, two days after a 'prime-time' special on default taxi's. It actually worked out in his favour. Everyone was ducking.

He has the plan and he's sticking to it, come hell or high water. Driving so long, he's seen a lot. Most of which he can countenance. Most things he's had an element of experience in. It is said four careers that involve psychotherapy are psychotherapy, writers, taxi drivers and bartenders. Clem started the first from a young age. His mother had had him at thirty-three. Following the birth of his sister four years later, she developed post-natal depression and went from there into menopause.

It was Tuesday, he'd call up to mum for a while.

"Will you collect me Saturday?"

"Yeah."

"What time?"

That day, when he picked the date, August seventh, everything really kicked off. Things happened, he made it public knowledge. He'd tell the family, his friends. He'd told them lots of plans before, dreams, schemes. Previous ideas were tied to rough dates, 'in the future', it was the first time he had a definite date.

For the holidays, he'd wanted to go to Buynol near Valencia for Tomatino, dressed up as Ron Burgundy. Mariella was relieved at seeing he wasn't coming. A terrible tension started growing all over her anytime it was near Clem's arrival. She found it hard to sleep, hard to eat, she couldn't stop thinking about him. Thirteen months, he'd be long gone, a distant memory from her mind.

It opened up another avenue for her, San Francisco. Her company had been scouting for people to send there for a year to learn English. Mariella was gregarious, outgoing and she loved adventure. She'd been holding back a little but this was her perfect opportunity. She'd clean him completely out of her system. She had been heading to the Cream-fields music festival in Valencia and offered him a carrot. It was the third time she'd done it. He'd bitten once but slipped away, he wouldn't bite this time either.

He was bi-polar, she knew it, she'd told him. "Who wants a mannequin?" he answered. She didn't. She didn't want Bi-polar either. She didn't know what she wanted. She loved his dreams, the lies he told her. He believed them so much, that she believed them, she knew they'd never come true. Was she thinking about him again? He'd written her the most beautiful poems. It took her a while at first, she had to translate them. Get help from friends with better English, they were amazed.

She'd received poems before from exes but not this good. She liked his name, the way it was different. It stood out. Mariella was drifting into thinking about him again. He'd come like a meteor and showed her the fakeness of her reality and let him turn the sincerity of a dream enter into her head. She'd promised herself to stop. She'd have to stop.

There was too much going on in San Francisco. Too much to live in the now, happening around her, to regret that she'd let pass while she was there. It seemed like she was becoming more serious, she was a woman now. Time to act that way.

He was the type that would never grow up, amount to anything.

She saw the direction her life was heading. It wasn't as romantic or dreamy as she'd first hoped but that's life, she was a woman. It was about getting on with it. She'd have her days. She didn't have time to be daydreaming about 'what ifs' and 'maybes'.

He was a weirdo, she'd let slip in. She hated him for his upside-down principles. The lack of them so often and then to find him stick solidly when she had him in her grasp. He could be so wimpy, panicky and then quite strong and stubborn. She walked all over him. He was a doormat and then inappropriately he'd find a spine, sending everything back to disaster mode. She liked that, he was tough.

Mariella closed her computer and went off to sleep.

Clem was examining himself constantly now. Smoking another cigarette, pulling into the all-night garage, where when the staff spotted his car, went straight to the coffee machine. Sometimes he wouldn't want the coffee, but the process had begun. Sometimes he'd say, "I don't want the coffee," but just a little less than never, he'd just take it. Had he become so predictable? Was his routine so 'Midnight Express' or 'Stepford'?

Wasn't there more to him? Would there be a day where assistants in the shop would say;

"That guy with the coffee… haven't seen him around in a long time! Did he die?"

"No, he said he was going to Spain."

"Wow! Did he make it? ...or is he dead?"

Or would Clem be like the Egg man. Clem hadn't seen him in years. The poetry of the wiry man with plastic bags so longing, straining in his hands to hit the ground as he plodded footpath after footpath. Clem could once have set his Saturday by him. He'd gone. Then about a year ago he was back. "That's him, the Egg man!!…" *'Bypass'* Clem thought to explain his absence. Greyer, still strong, the fight tougher, the steps harder, less fluent, breezes as strong as ever to face, harder to hold firm against. Always a grit in his teeth, his face a picture of struggle. Time had passed him by in many ways but he was still fighting. A throwback to fifty years ago, in today's times he was art.

Would he be like Emma, the girl who worked in the highbrow restaurant? A colleague of hers got in and Clem asked about Emma.

"How's Amy?" he always got her name wrong.

"Amy?"

"Emma," he'd correct himself.

“She’s gone, sure.” And that’s it ‘they’re gone,’ off around the world.

So many people say they’re going, you never really know who’s going until they are gone. Is it the same people all the time who say ‘they’re going?’. Does it just take between one or ten tries at it? Is it the same for ‘the loves who get away?’ Are they the same guys, the same girls? Does it just seem that way? What’s the whole thing about at all? He wondered, the equations, possibilities, destinies…

Is that just our minds? Why does he get spooked going for a piss behind the back of the car in the middle of the dark countryside or near a cemetery? How different it is when you’re on your own, sober. Why do you become so aware?

Why was he doing this? Why examine? So long, everyday, what was it worth to him? Is this the way to do it? He could hear himself calling to himself. *‘Stop Clem, Stop! That’s enough, no one wants to know, no one cares about these things.’* Clem would agree with himself for a while. And then other voices would come and say, *‘you might as well do it.’ ‘This is what happens.’ ‘This is what you have to go through.’* It’s strange, it’s weird, it’s lonely.

He’s doing it, another reluctant shrug of a shoulder. It’s fine once he starts, once he gets into it, it takes him away. He has his routine. Cigarettes, coffee, thinking, stream thought, stop, which thought now? This one for a while. Like landing in a new city. Looking for landmarks close to his hotel. Walking ever increasing circles to understand the local geography.

Socrates reportedly says ‘A’, Plato adds ‘A+a= B’ and so on. Pin pricking sources of knowledge without completely covering himself with references so scattered he would lose tremendous time organising them.

Saturday again, mother again. He starts off. Checks pockets, keys, walk, door, car, road, radio, park, door, door.

"Helloooo!" Clem enthuses.

"Ah, you're here. Hiya, Clemance," his mother responds in delight.

"I've been waiting all day for you," she says.

"Hiya, mam," he responds loud and cheerily.

She smiles again.

"C'mere til I want ya." She's reaching to her handbag for five euros to pay for the coffee. They argue until Clem takes it.

"Will you get the oxygen?"

"Yeah."

"Will you get a jacket?"

"Yeah."

"Will you get the five o' clock tablet?"

"Yeah."

"Will we be back for our tea?"

"Yeah."

"Where are we going?"

"For a spin."

"Okay."

Clem goes to her room and collects her things. As he puts the coat and the mobile oxygen tank around her, she continues her series of questions.

"Will we get the tablet?"

"Yeah."

"Will we get the coffee and the doughnut?"

"Yeah."

"Will we be back for five o' clock?"

"Yeah."

As he turns to drive out the questions keep coming. It gets to Clem and sometimes he gets a little snappy. He cools himself down thinking 'this too shall pass' in the knowledge it is far worse for her than for him. Snapping only makes the problem worse.

His father endured enough of it, realised it, but he just snapped more similar to Kate. It's hard though, hard. The patience of a saint is required sometimes. Clem admires the workers of the nursing home and though he has a slight minor misgiving about an odd member of staff, when you have to listen to her on all day, and for a euro above minimum wage it would be hard not to react.

A lot of the staff are saintly though, it is remarkable and Clem admires that greatly. The patience, the ability to understand, to be there and remain distant enough not to take it personally or let it upset them is amazing.

Clem does his duty. Time to unwind, a few hours in bed or a few in front of the television before work again. It is hard to make a jump, mental leap. To stay disciplined.

Chapter 5

'Luck,' the Equation

Strange how things are remembered after years of absence and then in a short period of time they are remembered again and again before they leave. The boy behind the bus was on Clem's mind again. He could feel him pulling and pulling for all his worth, the great fret as the cloth wouldn't release and the power of the bus would not relent.

Danger of the scrapes and fights. A bad, unlucky fall and that's it. That's all we are away from the end. Who deserves it? It's just math, bad equation for the individual. Who knows if you're going to fall in love with a bitch or a bastard? How do you know the history of someone, when they look hot, desirable? People gave themselves away in his taxi every night.

He had a well-designed seemingly ad-lib script formed at this stage and was able to prompt people with 'trigger words.' If the customer responded appropriately he would continue. He found a lot of people hungry to learn. That there was a world outside football, television, the weekend.

"There's a world outside football." Clem liked those nights when the customers were receptive to his ideas, they were sincere, genuine. Those nights were good. He felt good inside.

But the nights with the silence, the queueing, this was the hardest time. Where Clem could move ten metres in one and a half hours with only a radio or CD to listen to. This was the sameness. The sameness over and over and over again. Checking nothing on the internet, it was a reflection of the dark side of life.

He wrote sometimes. Smoked a cigarette or two but it seemed nearly every night he had to go through this. Time to contemplate his surroundings. Again, examine his life.

He assumed most people go through this. Was that a good enough reason for him to do it? *'No!'* Almost always dark, looking at the same streets, avoiding the same conversation with taxi drivers who were generally limited in conversation to the price of a fare 'from A to B', performance of the car, knew a lot about nothing, etc., pigeonholed, destroyed. They didn't want to be here either.

He was joining a street from a minor road one night and all along drove taxis with their 'for hire' lights on. It chilled him how it was like a cortege. Yet, there they were, just driving themselves to their own funeral. Waiting for what?

There were a few, who had lives or were on the way to lives.

December 16th, Clem hears of the death of Christopher Hitchens over the radio and he writes on his Facebook blog, "I'd love to have had a debate with him. We were of the same vernacular." He checks the word vernacular to see if his understanding of the word is correct. He's trying to impress Mariella, they're communicating again but he feels he has entered the world of the intellectual. It is forming and he is waving goodbye to a world of lesser talk.

He is driving, considering little. He has a quick look at the biography of Hitchens' life, his only previous reference being a couple of YouTube videos… which he found after traipsing the Foucault vs Chomsky debates. That bored him at first, so he stayed on Hitchens for a short period before quickly moving on to Carlin.

As he drove, because he'd already proposed the theory that 'time is indeed a loop' in his mind, that 'if there is no end to time, then why was there a beginning?' From this he came to figure religion as a place on a time chart along with God and the Big Bang theory. All the time, these ages, humankind has been taught heaven awaits but in fact it is now. That the miracle at all is that we got here. This is the benefit of all preceding events.

He also believes he understands Jesus Christ, near at 100 percent now. He feels he was a philosopher and that the 'kingdom of heaven' is here and now, right in front of people. He must have been thinking… "You idiots, do you not see this is it! Leave go of your fears, stupid taboos and inhibited life now." He must have been really angry about the blindness of man around him. He was of course misrepresented later on within an organisation that turned sour and corrupt.

It exists today, nearly as much, but the secret is out. Humanity has managed for a long time to keep a lid on things but with the growing ability of the individual to access the entire history of information with the internet, it is harder to hide the facts. From the year 2000 to 2005 the amount of people who believed in God dropped seven per cent from a figure in the high nineties. Clem also learns that the percentage of Swedes that don't believe in God is over seventy percent.

He needed to explore more. The information was at his fingertips but the experience of the facts was in the faces and words of everyone. He read a lot of people, heard what they said and would deconstruct what they were meaning. Quite often people said what they meant. They'd been programmed that way.

"What did you think of the match?" quite often meant, 'What did you think of the match?' not always, 'I'm bored and in order not to think too much about other things, I'm going to ask, how was the match, even though really it doesn't mean that much to me.'

Some liked going home, others didn't. Some would prolong conversations or repeat again what they'd said, trying to emphasise a point further. *'Keep going,'* Clem would think. Realising what faced some of them was the awfulness of whatever was behind that door. For some it was boredom and some loneliness. People, some to compensate, adored attention on a pet, like the pet gave too much of a worry for them.

Truth being known, the pets probably tended to care more than some people waiting behind doors. Clem was fairly patient. He'd the experience with his mother. Though being human, his blood could rise and boil, and often enough he'd be thinking, *'just get the fuck out of the car,'* but the diatribe would persist.

Often, he'd just sigh and look away somewhere distant, thinking randomly about different things, argue against the person's stupid statements in his head. He'd drive off thinking, *'what a dumb fuck.'* A lot of people were clueless on subjects that they were talking about, they just needed to talk.

Kate hated that about Clem. Clem talked crap too. They'd be discussing something ,and he'd come in with a completely irrational argument or a dumb statement that was completely wrong. *'Dumb guy, should have went to University. Everyone should go to University or they'll all just end up being mechanics or waiters or taxi drivers.'*

Clem had got so much more than Kate. Kate had to work her ass off. She was the eldest. She got the first wave of abuse at home. It focused in on her. The blame for her mother's deteriorating condition. She couldn't put up with that man. She'd have killed him or been killed.

She had to run, that time, when he'd just gone too far. Just too much, no one really knew what was going on but she couldn't take it, she had to leave. She moved to England and from there got a visa to Australia. She had done 'the nurse thing'. She really didn't even know if she wanted it but it was good, it looked well on the street and she received some peace for it but that didn't hold long.

Then it just kicked off. She knew so many contributing factors. The economy, him, her father at home all the time. Cooped up, nothing to do, led to the watching. Mother having to be a thrifty housewife. It was beyond her capability. She tried but she wasn't frugal enough, hard enough, mean enough. She was about spending money. She couldn't divide it, look after it, manage it over a long period of time. The bad budget, the poor food she had to buy, the second-hand clothes for the kids, the money for books, copies, clothes, sports, always hands, reaching out looking for money and her herself nowhere to find it. She was a mighty trier.

They were the eighties. That's what happened when redundancies were spent, that's what happened when people ended up staring at each other around kitchen tables or over armchairs and settees that were starting to grow old and decay and break. People get odd, people get angry. Kate saw it for what it was worth. It had been heading to this. She made mistakes afterwards, marrying a man too soft, a life of compensating. She had three children and loved them as any mother would, but she was left short changed.

The rest managed to stay. Why? Why were they able to stay? Has she borne the brunt? Whetted to a life of sole independence. Men unable to live up to any kindness or strength. Her children wouldn't turn out that way. Well, the first two anyway, Kate's youngest was a law unto himself.

Whatever was that child up to? That child, her brother. Why did it still annoy her? *'Him!'* Wild, finding trouble, mischief, when you'd talk to him you could see how sweet he was. He might have everyone else fooled but not her, in truth in conversations with the other siblings, they all agreed what Clem was, but they wouldn't do anything about him.

Kate had pointed out his flaws, his manipulations, delusions, yet he was still around, getting away with it, doing nothing. Why was she still fixated on it? Hadn't she enough on her own plate? Two divorces, three children. The good weather, holidays, university. Hadn't she had enough of home? Hadn't she broken free? She was gone eighteen, no… nineteen years now. And she still thought of it!!

And why did she go back? Why so often? When looking through the internet, falling upon cheap flights, *'okay with the dates, roughly'*. The pleasant memories of home, sweet times, overtook her. She presses 'accept' and it's done. She knows less than five minutes later she'll half regret it. The regret is more immediate. It's something to go through, a thing to get over again, before she can get back to things that don't bother her so much. Shoes! Why does she buy shoes that really she doesn't want, for them to let her down. Surely there are shoes that are great, perfect, she's found a few. Somethings work out better than you ever expect and other things let you down. The rest just fills in the time. She was going to phone Clem, tell him she'd booked.

Clem had been nine. There was a summer play scheme in the parish centre. He made a new friend for the summer, a wilder boy. Clem nearly felt dragged into the friendship but he was there now, so he stuck around. They were meant to go on an excursion but Trevor, who could cycle, who would later teach Clem, came up with the idea of 'truant'. They skipped the tour and went out to the countryside. After the fear of punishment and wrongdoing were far enough away not to matter, Clem opened up for a while to a whole new world of freedom. The heat from the sun was magnificent, when it broke through the showers, the sky was his, the grass was his, the roads were his.

They got back to Trevor's house before the community scheme closed and Clem walked the small distance home. Again, he'd been rumbled. Always caught, always Clem. His mother did the questioning and he lied for all his worth. Against everything that his mind was telling him to do. First thing, protect yourself! If he could expand the lies for long enough something would make them true.

It wasn't hard to see through his lies. He'd been ordered up to his room to think about what he did.

He thunk. What had let him down? This wasn't meant to happen. Wasn't God on his side? Why couldn't have God made what he'd been imagining true? Wasn't this what God was for? What was the point in being God if he wasn't going to do this for him? Is there something else stopping that God from being able to help?

Clem went to bed. He was really worried now. He'd messed up with his mum and maybe now he was messing up with God too. What a terrible day, after such a brilliant day, Clem hated Trevor. It was stuck. Who's God's boss? If God is God, who made God? He was weeping now. Why was he thinking these things? Why couldn't he stop? What would make it go away??

He fell asleep but the questions stayed in his dreams. He woke up at seven, the sun was still shining through the window, it was warm but Clem didn't really care, the sun didn't count for anything, it wasn't big enough to solve the God trouble.

Mary, his older sister, called up to tell him dinner was ready. She saw him crying. He didn't need to 'put it on', it was genuine.

"What's wrong, Clem?" she asked.

"Can I ask a question?" Clem had Mary down as the first in the ladder until he got to the adults. She'd had that invisible phone to Santa Claus too... Clem had become suspect over that but the authority line was so vast.

"Yeahhh," she said sweetly, gently sensing the delicacy of Clem's frame of mind.

"If there is a God, who made God?" Clem asked.

'That's one you don't get everyday,' Mary thought.

She came closer and stroked the mop of hair on top of his head. His mother cut his hair in a typical 'bowl style' that was deemed appropriate at the time. It also gave Mary a little time to think and how to phrase the question.

"That's where faith comes in!" Clem wondered whether it was the 'fate' fate, or the 'faith' faith, as he glued the rest of the sentence together. He'd got it.

"So he's like Santa Claus? Only bigger and realer!!" Clem answered with a great deal of relief. He hugged

Mary and gave her a big kiss. Everything could go back to the way it was. He'd go back to normal now. He never wanted to think about this, never again. It was all really Trevor's fault. He was going to be good again, good like God wanted him to be, good forever now.

Looking back through his life at any stage, even now, he recognises that as the worst day of his life. That horrible feeling of loneliness lying in the bed wondering about God. He'd often planned to think of it again but was more than happy to avoid it. *'Just don't go there'* was the best advice his mind had ever dispensed as he got closer to the subject. He'd do likewise as soon as he'd get on the plane for Madrid. Baggage happens, baggage will happen, look at it, examine it, make what you can of it, park it, let it go, move on, let's find some good things.

Chapter 6

Condemned to Mortal Dumbnation

'Just tug it, a quick whip and she's free.' He could see her convulsing, her face turning purple and to panic. Her eyes looking at him like he was destroying her. And then she knew. It was her time. He was freeing her. Soon, she would be dead, killed, euthanised. She wanted it. He had to do it.

For forty minutes since Clem arrived, she'd been 'on'.

"Will they put me on the chair?"

"Yes, mum," he responded.

"What time?"

"About five, when they come down with your tea."

"Will they put me down on the chair?"

"Yes, mum," answered again.

"What time?" she repeated.

Clem got up and walked around the room. It was a fair-sized pretty room, decorated with colourful gifts. For the five years her door was always open. It had been closed or less open recently. She'd been diagnosed with fibrosis of the lungs four years ago. Two years after that she could die at any time. November, it was at the advanced stage, the end.

The family, those that were around, agreed it was better that she remain in the 'bungalow' the name they used for the nursing home, rather than bring her up and down to the hospital, where she'd gone with an infection or pneumonia before. The stints were becoming more frequent, it wouldn't be long now.

She'd a strange life. A good life, a fun life, a suffering life. As the good and fun faded, the suffering had become omnipresent. Every time someone visited now, they could hear her calling for something, as they came down the hall.

She had been suffering a long time now. Thirty years of what Clem knew. Of what they all knew. It's different when it's family. It's really different, you nearly become a professional, at least a part of you does but it's always personal. Clem was balding, scruffy, slim, six foot and moderately handsome.

His mother when she was younger was one of the belles of the parish. His father, nearly five years dead, a local handsome sport star. Now she'd come to this, as bad again as the old days. He'd seen strange things back then.

"Will they put me down in the chair?" she asked.

Clem placed his cold hands tenderly on her palms. He stroked her lower arm. Her skin was flakey, dry, drooping more, the closer to her elbow it ran.

"Will they put me down in the chair?"

"Yeah," Clem answered.

"What time?"

"Around five."

"What time?"

Clem raised his eyebrows to no one. An invisible individual, the world as a witness. He rose and walked around the room. He needed to draw his attention away from her constant, trivial questions. He spotted the painting Kinga made for him. It had been three quarters hidden behind a stereo on the windowsill. He picked it up and looked at it. It was always nice to look at. It was nice that someone once, took that much time to think of him.

"It's lovely isn't it. A girl drew that for me." He said to his mother.

"A girl drew that for you?" she quizzed.

"A girl drew that for you?" she repeated automatically.

"Yeah mam, it's nice isn't it." Clem placed it centrally on the sill.

"Will they put me on the chair?"

"They will, mam."

"What time Clem?"

"Five o' clock, when they come with the tea."

"Will they put me down on the chair?"

Clem just nosed around a little. He wandered over to the sink.

"Are you going for a drink of water?"

"Nah, just looking around."

"Will they put me out on the chair?"

Clem didn't answer.

"Clem, Clem, look at me," her mouth and chin jaded in stress from talking.

He looked at the vase with pretty fresh yellow roses.

"Harry bought those," she called, stretching her eyeline uncomfortably.

"They're lovely, aren't they!" Clem answered.

"These are lovely too," he said pointing to a pot of red roses ready to bloom.

A brief silence. Twenty seconds maybe.

"Will they put me in the chair?" she called.

Clem walked over to the side of the bed and took her hand again.

The woman was suffering a terrible existence. He knew it. She didn't want to torture them, her children but that's what she was going through. Minute by minute torture.

He'd dropped a guy, a geriatric nurse, to one of the local hospitals that day. A reasonable musician waiting for his hangover to kick in.

"Went out for the one," he tried explaining.

"And you got to it in the end," Clem replied deadpan.

"I have to use that one," he said.

He asked Clem about the poetry, Clem told him it was out this week.

"Tough job?" Clem asked.

"Nah, not at all." He answered. "They have it worse than anyone."

"Yeah, you know my mother has dementia.

"And I remember being sick, at home from school and she'd bring up the tea and toast. Then she'd headed off in town for an hour, it was the longest time ever, waiting for her."

The guy, nodded in agreement.

'No one deserves this,' Clem thought. *'What a horrible way to die.*

'A quick flick of the oxygen tube, she panics, he grabs a pillow. She's in pain for a few minutes and she's free.'

"Will they put me down on the chair?"

"Yes, mum."

"What time?"

"Five o' clock."

'Just a quick flick,' cold, heartless or was it indeed the opposite? She was going to have to endure every minute of every day for however much longer she was going to be around. She wanted to die so many times before. She'd driven a car into a river, jumped from a top window, took umpteen overdoses. She was back in the state where she begged for shock treatment. The terrible hell was upon her again.

Clem had been in brilliant form. The 'hiya' from Dennis when he was sad. The justification for his life. The theory proven. His reason for living assured. Why he was here. What he was to do here. The sense of poignancy attached to it. All was going to be perfect from now on.

And this again. Twenty-five years on. Was he going to let the establishment rule again? The rule of law as opposed to justice. For the few sparks of happiness that came her way.

The memories came flooding back. Her, running down the hall of the geriatric ward, hands cusped, prayer mode, begging mode, crouching in front of Clem and his younger sister.

"Will they give me shock treatment?"

"Hi, mum," they'd say.

"Hi Clem, Hi Lorraine," she replied in the saddest most despondent tone you'd ever hear or see.

From the ages of twelve to twenty they'd been coming up here. Most times for a visit, sometimes the A&E ward, sometimes the I.C.U. department. They managed somehow, together, between them, live relatively normal years. They jumped characters. They turned out in ways to be dreamers, abstract, kind.

They'd look at each other and gave an acknowledgement, that there was something so wrong here. They needed each other to escape this and they drifted and created along with each other as crutches. Mealtimes were awful. Dad cooked terrible. No patience. The potatoes were always hard, cabbage watery, meat bland. He ate like a pig. He'd eat with a huge sound at the table. His jaws, once broken in a match, made a horrible noise like a dog cracking through a bone every time he chewed.

In fairness he cooked. Sometimes if they were alone, when he was in the kitchen, they were able to scramble some of it out through the window to the dog. Clem mainly lived on a diet of bread and butter those years. Soup was okay. His father didn't get better as he cooked through the years. Clem was a far better cook and in the evenings as they met in the kitchen he would cook 'special omelettes' that he and Lorraine enjoyed thoroughly.

Mum wasn't missing all the time. She'd recover and depending on circumstances she could be out for a long time. Sometimes she'd return not ready or rested or recovered at all and would find herself back in the hospital soon. Clem just loved being out of the house. Out in school, whichever girl's estate he was chasing at the time. Playing football, learning to drink from babies of vodka, whiskey or bottles of cider. They were all doing it. Well, some stayed home studying. Clem studied too.

He'd go to his room and close the book of what he was meant to be doing and would go off and work on an equation or write. Any whole number squared equals two times the previous number plus the previous number squared plus one. He'd thought he'd hit on something. It was nonsense, he was just getting by. He just drifted off into a simple world of math and writing, never studied what he was supposed to. He'd wing it in school. It was way too much later. He loved the now.

Cycling down a hill, standing on the pedals, to a place where people like him were. New people, where he was a mystery, for a while, and then next year he'd move on somewhere else.

"What time will they put me in the chair?"

"Five o' clock, when they come down with your tea."

Clem drew back to his mother. The sound of her questions again infiltrated his mind, the temporary solace.

"What time will the put me in the chair?"

Clem didn't answer.

"What time will they put me down in the chair?"

"Five o' clock, mum." *'Someone needs to give that poor woman morphine. Fill her up with drugs and just let her die peacefully. Or dish some hashish into her diet. You won't let a horse or a dog suffer like that,'* Clem thought.

'God, am I saying that again? I'll never say that again,' his mother thought.

"What time will they put me in the chair?"

'I'm saying it again. I'd be pissed off if I had to listen to me, God I hate being in this bed, God get me back in to the chair.'

"Five o' clock."

'He's answering me, I must be annoying, terribly annoying. I hate it in this bed.'

"With the tea?" *'Am I speaking again? I'll try and stop.'*

"Yes, mum," Clem answers.

'I wish I could stop. He's trying hard but it's just too much for him. I need to get out of this bed. My urine is gone again!'

"I'm wetting my pad, Clem!! I'm wetting my pad!!" *'How has it ended like this. It's going to run all over me, No! I've the pad. I've got to get out of this bed.'*

"Are you okay?" Clem asks.

'He's concerned, what a lovely guy, what a lovely son. I need to get out of this bed.'

"Is the pad on okay for you?"

She was once so fine. So loving. He remembers her tickling his feet or eating his cheeks. Lifting him up to the sink where he'd bend up his knees and dip them into the toasty warm water, with the suds all fluffy inside.

"Come here my little man!! Come here my little man!!" Clem smiled.

"What time is my tablet? Clemence?". She had drawn him back to the present, there was a strange feeling developing. *'To and from, drifting in and out.'* Why was she like this? She suffering, surely. Her mind had internalised to every second. Every small trivial matter had become exaggerated more and more until it grew to what it was now. A reverberating circle of immediate trivial thoughts that exercised themselves in request after request.

The next thing, the next thing, the next thing, is that what happens to people? Is that what's fed, sold? The opening lines of 'Existential' are quite eerie about the human condition of avoiding 'the now'. It's hard, how many of us have the proper conditioning for it? It's fearful in the greatest way. Clem was finding this out. He also correlated how the more rational he'd become or was becoming, the darker his mood set was.

For so long, he'd been dreaming, abstract, illogical, it brought with it a sense of lightness. The escape from reality. What reality is so barbaric that sends the individual of the species cowering?

'Why couldn't she die like dad? Drugged up to not even a consciousness? Rid of pain. She was heading, ultimately for a heart attack. A painful heart attack.'

Was her repeated 'next' a scream of hanging on? The groaning of pain from a stricken animal. Like the kicks skyward that strewn cat was sending. 'I don't want this? I don't want this? I don't want an end?'

Clem wanted to help. He'd seen Harry pass cigarettes and a lighter to his father on his death bed. The bed caught on fire one night. It wasn't allowed!! Harry still slipped him cigarettes but the rest didn't... it wasn't allowed. If Clem could, he'd drug her up the same way. If someone had a needle he'd inject her or should he bring his 'grass stash' with him next time and mix it in with something? He wasn't using. Something to just get her stoned. She'd been on meds for the longest time, but something to blow all that away. See her off to 'cloud land'.

Would Clem do it? Just a flick. Was that what he was here to do? Buck the trend, the ultimate, 'fuck you' to the 'you're not allowed', 'you shouldn't'.

"What time will they put me in the chair?" she asked another five times in a row.

She had the 'want' to die but the 'will' to live! While the 'will' was only an ember, the 'want' was overwhelming her now.

It was January 8th.

Clem flicked it.

Chapter 7

I Must Persist, Why Are We Here?

Why are we here?

We are here because this is heaven.

What is heaven?

Heaven is everything, in every line on a human face, every blade of grass, every grain of sand, every drop in the ocean. Every spring in a step or flap of a bird's wing, every laugh, every breath, every tear. Every physical, chemical and biological process.

Clem, afraid of plagiarising others and in the process tainting himself, decides it is okay to do a little more research. He looks at some more of Hitchens' work and checks out Dawkins' as well. He uncovers that scientists are working on the theory of time that there may have been a contracting universe before the Big Bang, which applies more validity to his current developing theory that time may indeed be a loop.

He ponders that if time is so vast, then what we have thought could be plotted on a chart. Where's heaven? When did it come into existence? Where's God? Where's the Big Bang? He thinks for a second. Does the Big Bang belong to 1958, when it was discovered, or the very beginning? He concludes it belongs in two places, 1958 and the beginning, but in his theory that's anywhere around the time of God's first appearance, God belongs roughly around 40,000 B.C., they both start off at the very start and 1958 and 40,000 B.C. when humans first thought of God but in Clem's chart, the start could be anywhere. Time just as it goes on now, with no end would have had no beginning, no beginning with a relevance to humanity and no end to it likewise. He also learns that this is close to Hubble's theory, which was later disproved. Which leads Clem to a new theory or question: maybe there have been many beginnings and there will be many ends?

He studies the string theory of nine dimensions being interrupted by a tenth which caused the start of the universe.

It seems the question of how we got here will go on a lot longer than why we got here. But why we are here, is because 'this is heaven' no eternal damnation awaits. We don't live on, though whatever we create does, for a while at least.

It being near to Christmas, he went out with a few friends for a drink. He was driving, so it was necessary to keep the drinking down. He'd two pints of Guinness and six glasses of coke for the evening. They asked of each others' families and discussed philosophy and poetry, as opposed to football. Such a different conversation than they would have had five, ten or fifteen years earlier.

Paul was there, a local chief fire officer, 'famous for being on TV' the joke of the night. Clem had been told recently by Patrick, a fan of Clem's poetry, that Paul was big into philosophy. Neither had known this about each other. The death of Hitchens provided the solid ground for the two to approach this subject.

Having previously not got on like bosom buddies within the dynamics of the group, they had a few 'odd words'. Firstly, they were interrupted by an old friend who really did not permit such a conversation on philosophy, God, etc., she went away and as Clem looked around at the uniforms of Fred Perry and Ralph Loren shirts, *'you judging people again, Clem?'* he heard himself in the back of his mind. Eventually four of them gathered round.

"Christopher Hitchens died!" Clem announced to the group, solely aimed at Paul.

"I'll miss him," Paul said.

"Who's he?" Marty quizzed.

"A philosopher, writer," Clem answered. It meant nothing to the others.

Victor and Marty looked on. This was Clem, *'he's weird, he does that,'* they'd never known it was Paul, Clem hadn't known it was Paul either. Clem knew Vic and Marty were 'straight up' guys. It was mutual, neither thought less of the other, pure acceptance.

"Religion?" Paul asked.

"It's a crock!!" Clem answered.

"Yeahhh," Paul laughed in agreement. Like they'd faced up to something they weren't meant to.

"God?" Paul asked further.

"Santa Claus, for grown ups."

"Yeah," Paul giggled again. Victor and Marty looked on, as if they, Paul and Clem, knew something, really knew something, when that older child comes along in the schoolyard with some new information. They were able to deal with it, together, by themselves, like marriage or fatherhood or death.

Clem guessed a lot of it was Paul's job. Paul would have seen a lot. Floods, car crashes, fires. Life, then corpses. Life, then corpses. Where does it go? Nowhere really. It just ends.

They agree in principle it should be taught, religion, until something better comes along. As a history, of how it manipulated but as a guideline to good moral living. The 'self' benefits from such restraints.

"Hmmm," they said in unison.

“For a while anyway,” Paul answered. That was for another day. Tonight was about enjoying. There is a great freedom in that. To let go. To enjoy the now. What’s troubling you will still be there tomorrow but the ‘here and now’ has to be embraced when it comes along.

For guys around the forty mark they really lived it up. For the years of Clem’s misbehaving he’d become the quiet one. He was driving anyway.

Victor and Clem discussed each other. There had been a discussion about Patrick a few months earlier. Patrick, Victor, Marty and Clem. Patrick was in a predicament, according to who? or what? was Clem’s defence. He was defending himself through Patrick. He’d had trouble on this issue before.

“How do you do it, Ban Ban?” (a nickname for Clem) Victor asked.

“I dunno,” he answered. “It’s just me,” he shrugged.

“Of all the people, I never thought you’d still be around,” Victor said. Clem shrugged again.

“How do you do it?” He wasn’t disparaging, just curious.

“Do you have a pension?” he continued.

“Surprisingly...sort of,” Clem replied.

“There’s five of us here tonight, and the four of us, we’re all married.” Victor’s wife was midway through pregnancy, so he avoided that. He was safe, he was fair, he was kind and extremely witty, tonight he was a little profound, *‘maybe that’s impending fatherhood’* it grated a little with Clem, just a little, it wasn’t delivered that way or intended so. Just that he was still where he always was and the feeling that he might have missed the boat did visit him.

"I just want something different, I don't know what it is yet but I just don't want this. I don't think I do. The path of cradle to grave, finding myself in something I don't want," he extended. It dawned a little on Clem that all those things, that he didn't want, hadn't happened but really not much at all had happened.

He could see how on the outside, looking in, how it seemed he could be 'stuck', it was so long now. The move to Spain had passed through his lips so often that it would have bored people to death by now, but he persisted. He was going to stick to it. Whatever that would bring.

"How the old fellas were right!" Victor spoke.

"Huh?" Clem answered.

"How the old fellas, knew so much... when we were younger," Victor continued.

"Em!" Clem answered, had had this argument in his head before, *'how they weren't so right at all, in so many things'*. He was thinking which argument to select from or whether there was a reason… *'Victors' talking.'*

"We were in New Zealand."

"Really, I didn't know that," Clem responded.

"For our honeymoon."

"You'd been down that way before," Clem prompted.

"Yeah. The difference was huge. Instead of being drunk all the time, it was nice to sit and watch the marvel of the place. In the fullness of time I'd love to go back but when I was there, I was thinking this could be a once in a life time thing. I might never get back here again. I soaked it up," Victor shrugged his shoulders, it was an honest gesture communicating life, it's grandeur, it baffled Victor too. He was happy though, as the rest of them, as they could be, as happy as life allows.

Clem knew they'd come visit him in Spain. He'd have to get there first but there would be a day. They'd come into his bar and they'd drink the house dry. It would be a good day. But in his mind he couldn't help thinking about the scene from *Educating Rita*, when she was in the pub and they were all around singing. Clem would have to sing later that night. That song he hated, that song he wrote all those years ago, but there wouldn't be too many renditions of that left here.

This should have been more poignant. Rita left the pub because she just didn't belong there anymore. This group had gone its own way a long time, spread out. Attune to their own thing. It had never been a suffocating or overly tender group, just average, but it was their group. Clem could see himself leaving the scene, it was happening.

The friends got drunk and rude, well a couple of them. Clem was happy, giggling at some of what they got up to. They sang loudly in places they shouldn't have, Clem gave his rendition, and they went to a late teens disco where they were old enough to be everyone's father. The same bouncers worked the doors though. They were shaking hands as they went in. That was strange. The streets were full, was it the same in other groups?

Clem drove them home, to their wives, to their houses, to their lives. It was fine. He didn't work that night, he just went home to bed, he enjoyed it for what it was but looked forward to next year.

Chapter 8

Losing Ground

The fundamental differences between right and wrong, pure right and pure wrong.

Having a conversation with a friend who has so much more than Clem, materially, socially, in terms of the American dream and probably a little healthier due to choices of lifestyle. There it ends, his friend believes 'this is hell', he's far from the only one, 'there has to be something better after this' but the rational side of him, agrees that the probability of 'there being something better' is slim, he holds on to it though.

Peter, the friend, waits twenty minutes for the lift, he is, more was, a good friend. He opens the conversation on familiar lines. He knows Clem writes. He knows Clem wrote twenty years ago. Peter is with his wife, Sharon, a really lovely pleasant woman.

Clem, pitches through the small talk. It's Peter, it's Clem. Whomever he's asking about is irrelevant. School people. Clem knows they don't give a monkeys, why should they, they are no longer a force relevant to their lives. Peter wants to stay there a while, in the nostalgia.

'A conversation with Clem can be hard. Funny but hard, inspiring, hopeless. It's on, it's God. What really is all this, anything for?' Peter ponders sometimes, on his own, *'no one else he can really talk to about this except Clem?'* Clem doesn't go for the trivial. Friends from the earliest days. They have separated as individuals. They have different value systems.

Clem explains his current theory. It bothers Peter. *'Clem! heart of gold Clem! No God for him? Where does that leave the rest of us?'* But Clem has changed, he's neither five nor seven or ten or fifteen, his positivity still sounds so certain. *'Here he is driving a taxi, no woman, still living in the house he grew up in, still dreaming,'* Peter, like so many others had seen Clem spout on for many years. 'Billy Liar,' so many different 'he's going tos!!' and nothing ever changed. Peter ended up okay. The economy was hurting but he'd looked after his money, there was pressure but he'd get through.

Peter's mother died in his teens and his father a few years later in his early twenties. Clem went in a neighbour's car to the funeral, with the same brother who was there in the convent for the biscuit episode. Clem thought it was something, to be there with him but he knew it was complete narcissism, he didn't know then what it was. *'Look, I'm comforting!'* or *'in a position to comfort!'* Clem doesn't get that, doesn't understand that now. He knows he was only fourteen or fifteen but was there so much missing from his life back then? Is there still a lot missing? Was there such a lack of attention missing he craved through his life? He wasn't there, at the funeral, for 'the sake' of it, he wanted to care. That moment crept in, he felt ashamed of himself for it.

Peter had a great relationship with his father. His father was a bright man. Clem knew him fondly when he was smaller and had a conversation in 1991 about things. He was never angry, well he was, *'only an odd time,'* Clem remembers coldly. But he was a decent kind man. Then Clem's own father never got cranky in front of the neighbours. Clem realised, at points of life along the way, he was behind. He was quicker still than his friends in a math problem or a line of wit. But as they passed on from another stage of development, Clem wasn't quite done, he was fine with that. He'd seen 'the end game' at home, he wasn't in a rush to get there.

Peter's dad basically died from a broken heart. That's how it went. There is no rational argument to say to someone, "stop being in love with someone who is dead." As sad as it is, from a personal standpoint as opposed to a logical one, there is really little in life as beautiful as certain kinds of love of the human heart and mind. Why then is it rational to have an argument with someone who loves 'a God' in the same way? *'Hmm, interesting.'*

Clem dropped four twenty-year-old lads home to the countryside. He collected them once and they immediately took to him. It was like someone from the older generation understood. They had smoked a few joints but were reverting to their more alert side as the 'high' wore off. They, like Clem, would be emigrating, just waiting for their degrees to come to a finish.

Clem had been thinking, earlier that evening, in response to a question posed by Peter, on the existence of the paranormal, "how do you explain the existence of that?"

In the meantime, he'd met Stephen, who wanted to become a detective in the police force. He'd been having a discussion with his friends about the right of self-defence when a burglar enters a house. Stephen just passed twenty one and liked his music. He played guitar and wrote. He'd got to perform on stage in a summer festival, a true highlight. Clem used to get breakfast for a while in the shop where he worked. Five o' five, the cost of what Clem spent every morning. Stephen had got his number, when he needed a taxi, that was nearly two years ago.

Clem didn't come for breakfast anymore. It was the sausages, he'd just got fed of them. How predictable he'd become was the truer factor.

Clem had asked Stephen to join him for a recording session when he got around to it. He'd picked up the guitar over a year ago and played songs he'd recorded on his phone. He was still way off a decent standard but was getting better. Stephen agreed to the request but since the first time he'd asked, eight months had passed. Stephen was concerned with his own goings on. His boss was turning out to be constantly annoying, forever watching, forever behind his back or over his shoulder.

The world has some of these people, not as many as one would think but when they're on you, it seems that everyone is on you. These people who make a minute seem like an hour, and an hour like a day. It poked out, joining a chorus of similar voices that stretch back further than one can remember.

Stephen said the first question asked in philosophy class was, "if you didn't have anything, what would you have?" the class responded, "you'd have nothing" with which the professor answered, "how can you have nothing?" Clem and Stephen continued on the rights, wrongs and law of the burglary case. Stephen asked Clem the question as they entered his housing estate, by the time he'd left, Clem had sent a text, "The birth of the universe."

Connor, one of the four twenty-year-olds, was asking about things he'd done in his twenties. The first time, Clem had told of some of the events, which the lads found shockingly funny.

"What are the roads like?" Connor asked.

"Lovely," Clem replied.

He'd said "tarry" to Peter on the Saturday night when he asked the same question.

They were talking about women at first, and the hypothesis that one having sex with a girl on a one night stand was a lot to do with more 'one for the boys' than for the intimate pleasure that can be devolved from such practice. Connor was on about Thursday night and he met a girl in a club, she invited him home. They were getting undressed, when she asked him, "do you have a condom?"

"Are you not on the pill?" he asked.

"No," she said.

Clem is thinking, *'have women already given up at this stage too? Are they thinking "I'd better, because…"?'*

"Get one off one of your friends," Connor said was her response.

"I went to the jacks (toilet) for a piss, and put on my clothes and headed away," Connor concluded.

"Yeah, I've done that too so many times. Do I really want to do this… with you?"

Clem gesticulated. Clem had been to bed with a lot of women, had sex with a small percentage. The stimulation died quite quickly for him, unless she was feisty, fiery, was that a fault of his prowess? The exaggeration of his thought process, his catholic upbringing, too much alcohol? Before he'd compared some sex to a level just above necrophilia, maybe he was no good at it, in bed anyway. He found stimulation much easier in a crowd, or in the open or strangely enough after a prolonged period of tenderness and comfort. Sometimes in the middle or just before sex with a particular female, his mind would enter a strange, abstract trance-like zone. He'd just drift off, get bored.

He knows that the problems of libido are as much the environment, as a man's mind. How can you say to a woman the things inside your mind, like, "when I met you I didn't realise you'd have this much fat... it's getting to me a bit." "Your shoulders are really big." It passed through those minds that rejected him too. But it happened with really pretty girls too. It took him a while to get going with a gorgeous Portuguese girl Floribella. He was thinking of a football match that had happened such a long time ago, he just couldn't get it out of his mind but then Floribella had her own solutions.

They spent seventy-two hours straight in bed together. Clem had to go to work to collect his cheque. Clem would call back that evening, he never came back. What was that about him? He wasn't ready?

As he drove the lads along the back road, the question opened up onto religion. One lad had been dropped off at this point. The other three claimed they didn't believe in God.

"Already, you don't believe in God!!" Clem claimed agog. "But ye're only twenty, is it a fashion statement? How did ye come upon such a conclusion already?"

"Because of evolution, because how is God everywhere?" they claimed.

Clem pulled over to the side of the road and asked the front seat passenger to read what he'd written just prior to picking them up.

> "So, to explain the possibility of ghosts and other paranormal existences, if it exists, maybe there were supplementary Big Bangs. Maybe there was a shotgun effect, and though the universe was born and sent forth in such an expanse maybe there are 'lagging pellets', time before us,

and ‘forging pellets’, time advanced, in the factor of the whole. Time warps? As the universe is one giant equation:

Earth + Mars + Sun + Moons etc., = Universe.

And:

Ocean + Land + Humans + Grass + Atmosphere = Earth.

Isn’t the result of splitting an atom, a series of more divergent equations. Where, like at birth, these equations are already there! It’s necessary for a specific series of conditions and circumstances to exist? Everything may be predetermined by the existence of an equation, that though still running as time progresses, the equation at any past point becomes predetermined!!”

Clem was just a bit weird. They never rang him again.

Clem needed to surmise.

“God or no God?

No God.

Heaven? No heaven.

Big Bang or no Big Bang? No Big Bang!!

Really… Why are we here? Don’t know yet.

How did we get here? Evolution.

Where does the species go from here? Extinction or space.

Why are you here? I don’t know.

Why are you here? Because I haven’t figured out what to do with my life yet.

You’d want to get a move on.

That’s why I’m here!

Fair enough.”

Why is God so important? When man couldn't come up with an answer God was the 'Joker'. He was the giant 'X' in every equation. From an individual's perspective, it was the reason for him doing something. It was the reason something happened to him, it was why he was here. So without the 'God', or giant 'X', there is a lot of explaining needed. Probably… yes, but why don't we use a 'Y' instead, in the meantime? A giant 'Y'. Same sound as 'WHY'. Let's just tip away at that until we find out more stuff.

So what's an individual to do, if God isn't the reason for doing something? Well, let's point people off toward Maslow. We've got basic needs to meet. After this, it's what's being pedalled by whatever market conditions prevail in a certain jurisdiction or society. A lot of it is false but because it's there, it's real. The difference it makes to an individual decreases the more they possess. After that, it comes back to their mind, their very own state of mind.

Clem feels that the old subject history should be taught differently. Not as a matter of fact, but what happened because of specific circumstances during events, to a point, they hold merit but the emotional consequences of leaders, soldiers, populous, cultures and beliefs.

The first subject that should be taught is 'panic'. This is what happened when such a General got the spooks. It led to complete devastation. This is what happened to such a tribe who thought, 'Three hundred soldiers with spears plus God was better than Three thousand soldiers plus guns.' The enemy never has Gods.

Clem is a romantic though. He doesn't want the species to bow to the odds. He doesn't want to turn snivelling. He doesn't negate that at some point the dour dog has his day. Yes, many don't but sometimes the equations favour him, it's just knowing which one to get on. One can wait forever, that's the thing, one can't.

There are two YouTube clips that resonate with Clem on this matter. Both of turtles just hatched, scurrying across the beach to make it to water. They both make it, safety, life. Just at the end of one of the clips, a big, winged bird plucks one of the turtles from the sea. Neither turtle knows in advance what lies ahead. Both are born and run.

Humans are a little more complex but the consequences of the runs are as open to other factors as that which face the turtles. No matter how long you wait, it is innate in us to run, one day, just to run. Some wish to run but for whatever reasons never run. Fear, frustration, duty. Others run too soon, because they panic, some get burnt, some of them survive in the 'sameness'. Others, funny ones, are born running, they are beautiful, they just run and run and run. Clem runs in circles.

Yes, he's pushing himself but it requires that. There is no God doing it. The Olympics, watching the weightlifters, runners at start lines go through so many psychological preparations, opera singers, actors getting 'in character', it's a human thing.

Clem has seen it work. And as he retraces his steps, he wonders what he was really up to, as opposed to what he seemed to be up. He nearly always lives in the future, so many people do, generally the optimists can't stop, 'runners' for the lack of a better word. Hence, Clem proposes pessimists live in the past. Rueful, regretful, yearning for better old times. The 'Now'. Clem likes the 'now'. Not necessarily the now 'now' but the 'nows' he's had. He will return to that state, he's looking forward to more ‘nows’, more ‘beautiful events’ and he plans to take them in and embrace them.

All this was changing Clem. He’d notice it more and more as he’d go along. In order to answer a question he was figuring out what the individual was saying. Digest the information, deliberate and come back with a reasoned solution or a further question, if he needed more detail. He remembers in maths, the ‘sums competition’, who could answer quickest. Twenty-three minus seven? Brain computes, answer, through to the next round. Fourteen multiplied by nine? Brain computes, answer, through to the next round.

The final was always three others, Clem was there, except once or twice, words stuck on the way out, or a different thought would stream in, anything at all, bird, stars, the numbers moving around, anything, interrupting the calculation.

The same three would come up against him, rotating. Forty-five plus sixteen minus eleven? Brain computes, answer, win. He lost a few finals too, not many but a few. Why was that thing inside running out to answer, to speak, to win? Like the loudest chick in a nest?

English spelling, grammar, they were too messy, it had to be remembered, learnt. Poetry was different though, making it up, that the words at the end ‘landed’ to be the same sound as the one above it. The teacher wrote it in big black marker against a shiny gleaming white laminated board. The teacher put the sun shining high, it seemed happy.

School was school. Being there with others, being in your own mind, being there with things. He liked school, more than the days he didn’t like school. It was rarely harsh and he had a few days of glory, scoring the winning penalty after the drama of the longest drawn out match ever. He really loved playing.

Chapter 9

Do You Really Want to Go There?

Clem, earlier in the night had been reading Dante's *Inferno*, he'd read part of the poem and decided that Dante was dealing with a 'de factum' God. This was really a hinderance to where he could go. Was he indeed laying out a work for later, to be interpreted by a world, politically and socially, where God or the politics of God were not such an influence on art?

Clem, from an early age, had decided that education was not so much in the works of others but by the world around him. People's faces develop similar patterns, their behaviours are routine, as indeed was his own. Many a day he spent regarding ants and insects plough about their daily business.

Clem carried on with Dante's *Inferno*. It was a quiet night. The only conversation of note was with a pretty woman who originated from China. She worked in a religious shop, the topic brought up because Clem had yet to begin his Christmas shopping. The previous year, she told that three baby Jesus' were stolen, so this year they had to tape him down to the crib. One man bought all his presents Christmas eve late last year. She suggested Clem could do the same.

She opened up to Clem, after he'd prompted, how she was not catholic or even Christian.

"Me neither," he responded. "So," with a carefree wave of his hand and a non-judgemental shrug of his shoulders he asked. "What religion are you?"

We were brainwashed." She claimed with a nice accent.

That when she was in China, the first thing they made them do was write the words, “The government is great” ten times.

“We were too!! We went to a convent… we still are,” Clem responded.

Later affirmed without persuasion, by a slightly older man on the way to the train station.

Dante’s inferno fascinated him. It didn’t fascinate him as much as it scared him. Was he prepared to say things that would get him a bullet? Climb that mountain. Make him unloved, unpopular. He thought Dante a tad cowardly. Clem was exactly where Dante was, Dante had to know there was no God. Was Dante playing to the crowd?

It was astonishing for Clem. How, many people were coming out. Non-believers. No God, simple as. Not horrible people, indeed very nice, interesting, inquisitive people. He felt like he needed to get them to a room or a field at this rate. We don’t have to be ashamed anymore. We can build a new constitution.

He gave credit that night to the western world. Kim Jong Il had died. He realised that those in North Korea had no access to information and the information they were being fed was total propaganda. Clem was afraid of himself espousing the conspiracy theory. The western world had given him the freedom to debate openly with others on such subjects that were taboo to him as little as ten to fifteen years ago.

He figured those that remained in the ‘I don’t want to know’ category would follow suit as soon as the tide turned.

Vaclav Havel died. The Czech leader had been a playwright. He influenced the world for the better. Seen the 'velvet revolution' through without bloodshed. Clem once had a thing about Czechoslovakia. It was one of the places his finger ended on, in the atlas. His father loved war documentaries, *The World at War* was a remarkable series. He wanted to write a book one day about a woman. A woman who had seen her husband dragged off to the first world war and her son the second. He wanted to overlap something but he only ever got a few pages into it.

He'd been to Prague seven years earlier. Met Jana one Saturday night in a club near Charles Bridge, it was one of the few times he hadn't wandered off from the group when they went away on such weekends. He hung around for the night with Jana, her cousin Lenka, and Lenka's boyfriend. She was an absolutely stunning blonde. Clem got her e-mail and promised vehemently he'd write her and make it back one day.

The relationship grew via e-mail for two years and the last e-mail was sent four years later. He sent her a few poems and short stories, they were bad work, but back then, for a while, Jana held court with him. He'd promised her many times to come to Prague, and she was looking forward to him coming, but he never had enough money to go. He was still gambling, gambling as bad and losing as heavy as always. It just died and he forgot about her even though he remembered things about the Czech Republic. Masarik, Milan Kundera and mushroom soup… Kuchta, and *pess*.

As Czechs and Slovaks migrated to Ireland, he had a head start in building a common bond with them. That would offer him one real alternative to Mariella.

Clem knew it was easier now to be an atheist, how quick the information spread. Only six years since Hitchens' *God is not Great*, four since Dawkins' *The God delusion,* he was thinking that the only thing absent was a doctrine. An atheistic doctrine. Plausible for logical thinking. He'd enjoyed the Chomsky vs Foucault debates second time round, liking Chomsky more. Perhaps he, Clem, should write it?

Perhaps he should start with his own, for his own personal reasons without ramming it down people's throats like the way it had been for millennia. Just do it, put it out there. The deaths of Havel and Jong, two more striking characters dying simultaneously could not have offered a better example to him. A question he'd have to check was, what was the perspective of the world according to Jong, the history of it. To him had he done the best for his people? According to him? Or just abused power for his own gain?

Clem started to click, 'the philosophy of Juche'. So there was an internal squabbling of ideological differences in the sixties between the Soviets, Chinese and North Koreans. Differing opinions were surfacing in the west too. Washington protests, hippie movement, Paris riots!! *'Let's read on'*, Clem thought. Agitation department… got to love that, and Jong owns the entire series of James Bond!! He forced bureaucrats to work amongst civilians for one month a year.

Flood, then famine devastates land. Placates army first. A swallow tells of his birth, turns Godlike. Clinton offers two nuclear stations for energy purposes. 2002 a U.S. intelligence crew find he's secretly enriching the country with Uranium…

Alarm bells! 2002, U.S.? Bush? What is the whole story here? Really?

Clem goes to bed. He lays in the bed. He understands he has to follow this in order to figure out the reasoning. Again, not a conspiracy theorist but he understands behind many protocols, ulterior motives, they may be rife.

He lays down, takes a look at the stock market prices, down a dot. The bed is warm but his feet are covered by the least thickest part of the quilt. He smokes a cigarette.

'Why am I trailing through this information? There are minefields, nuances and hidden agendas that are going to bring me around in a lot of circles.

'Aren't I meant to be looking for God? Or why I'm here?' he streams. "A thought, exists!" Clem claims in the bed, "even if that thing never exists, means it existed."

'So there is a God even if there is not a God! If someone has thought it, then it has existed, I have thought of 'God' as real before but he, it, only existed in other minds was betrothed to me. If no such entity had ever entered a mind, what would we have? There had been real Gods, well, with a touch more physicality. Like even now, Jong!! It's a manipulation of other minds. We manipulate our own minds. Or do we? Is it other forces, equations, is it a thread? Is there a genetic necessity in a mind to have it create something new? Or do we assemble new thoughts from an integration of other thoughts?'

'Why are there some things you can do, that you 'can't do'? and other things that 'you can't do' that 'you can't do'? and things again as an individual 'you can't do that you can do?'

Clem reasons, one, in a way, can surrender their mind to manipulation. Sometimes it can be very rewarding, 'going along with the flow', then finding a stop, personally, to get off. Many of these stops can be a lot more attractive than they turn out to be but there is always a flow, always a way back, even if the flow is different when one returns.

So what was Clem's flow? Well, he's in the flow of the western world. Probably the best flow to be in. The flow of paying the basics, it's why he works the taxi. The flow of falling in love because it was, is, the thing to do. The flow of falling out of love because it was not the thing, he or the other party wanted.

The flow of trying to buy a house, sort of, but that remained a farm, or a ranch in Spain, that he could turn into a studio. The flow of having children? Yes, because they're lovely and cute and great and it's the thing to do, if one is lucky enough to be able to do it, but no, because he'd have to do a lot of the work that comes along with that, of which he wasn't prepared to do freely at this time.

What was Clem's favoured flow?

He'd have to figure that out but back to God vs. Thought, and what were Bush and Jong up to? But first… and then Clem's feet were warm and he was asleep.

Clem didn't sleep long, his mind was active. He went to research the Bush versus Jong subject.

Bush was right, according to Clem's research, the C.I.A. had uncovered Jong's plans. Jong and the North Korean authorities plain admitted to it. In his distant memory Clem recollects the incident and pictures it in his head. He uses the images from Fukushima, the recent Japanese nuclear power plant that had been destroyed in the Tsunami and jets flying from a photo library somewhere he'd seen on television, both images were completely inaccurate but it worked.

Bush, so wrong about Iraq, Weapons of Mass Destruction at the very least, and so right about North Korea.

What games were at play here? What were the masses not privy to? Did it matter?

The population of North Korea deluded into believing that Jong was a God. The Muslims deluded that Mohammed was the saviour. The Christians deluded that Jesus Christ was the son of God. The Jews that Abraham was their leader, plagiarised upon the Egyptian gods, originally taken from the sun, the stars and the planets.

What are the modern day delusions? Run a marathon? Be rich, famous, wealthy? Clem had run a lot and the great feeling he got from running was diluted by the lack of fanfare. No champagne corks' popping, or wreath to wrap around his neck. No confetti falling from the sky or the ceiling when he got home. You have to make it somewhere in order to get those plaudits, that gratification. It might work for some but that wasn't it for him. He could sense the pleasure and fulfilment of a marathon runner running in a marathon.

He didn't go for X Factor, he took an odd look to see if a song he liked would come along. The melodrama was so plain but he'd little choice on television when he looked at it. The storm had knocked out the satellite months ago and it had only four colours left. It suited better. The previous year he moved it into the living room, to lessen the distraction. He'd wished he'd the power of mind to do it solely by will, but he'd lapse, and an hour a day would again become five or six.

How often he'd get up to go work and the feeling of wasted time would overcome him. 'Vicarious living!!' for all his rhetoric, he knew he was corrupted inside. If it wasn't television, it would be gambling, drinking or golfing. What was he indisputably running away from? What part of himself existed that he didn't want to know about?

For once an earnest effort to face it. Himself, alone, honestly.

Was it him? A force greater than him? Or was it the way he'd been developed by the environment around him?

Chapter 10

Condemned to Mortal Dumbnation

It might be no good just sitting there but it's nice to have it around if you need it or want it.

Clem got up early, three in the afternoon, sleep had been rough and he knew he had to get back to the subjects he'd been discussing in his mind before he went to bed, 'Jong, Bush, God, Flow, ya De ya da!' first, coffee and a cigarette. The house was cold. He didn't want to put the heating on. Money was one thing but it did little good downstairs. The house was badly insulated. So he'd wear his big black leather jacket, hood over his head, in the kitchen, waiting for the kettle to boil.

He didn't mind the dark, not this much of it though. Always dark. He liked the sunrise and sunset. He was going to be so out of tune with the heat in Madrid. He'd worked in a greenhouse for nine years and he kinda liked the 'sweat factory' heat of the place in the summer. A breath of fresh air would be so welcome in the Julys and Augusts of Madrid.

Clem returned to lay in bed, thinking of three conversations which overlapped each other. The talk with Stephen on 'why does God let kids get raped?' … 'But it is man who rapes the child.' Clem comes to a quick conclusion that nature doesn't give a shit about man, floods are floods. It doesn't know whether it's killing animals, humans, insects, it's just one giant math equation that happens. It doesn't know who it is killing either. A prime minster or a criminal.

The Earth doesn't care about humans or does it? Is it indeed a living thing? *'Let's consider this.'* Humans create huge, huge spaceships. They are self-sufficient! Using solar energy or whatever modern advances are made over the next generations. They bring on board whatever other species are relevant to human existence and survival, and over the course of so many years they travel so far away that the Earth becomes irrelevant to them, those humans. Does it matter then what happens to the Earth? The Earth implodes or man destroys it, something happens that wipes out life?

If there is life out there, in the far reaches of outer space, is it meaningless? Like emigration from years ago. When one left a land, to go to another, did one exist to the land behind anymore? Outside certain parameters, did the mother country which one left have any bearing on future generations? Perhaps a DNA imprint, a sentiment value but how relevant? Maybe future ghettoization but that is now to be expanded from in the new environment. As the new environment impacts more and more on the individual, less of the original country's resonance remains.

Like if we were fish and crawled from the sea, we don't really need to swim anymore and we don't need gills. So if we trip off into space, does the Earth remain a living thing? Things live on the Earth?

Humans need the Earth. Humans need the Earth for the foreseeable future. It would be hard to build spaceships for seven billion people. Humans are at the mercy of the Earth and each other. It may be a host to life, along with the energy from the sun of living things, and currently the main controller, but the shift of that premise, is possibly changing.

If evolution is such, why don't all other species want to evolve into humans?

Clem is again stumped, uncertain, he goes off to the internet. Is evolution true? He's already thinking, *'if not, how did we get here?'* More research, later. Clem goes to work.

"Why do I keep doing that?" Clem shouts at himself. He'd dropped a Spanish gent at the airport early in the morning. They talked generally in Spanish and had a good conversation on the journey. Clem asked in Spanish, "My Spanish is not too bad?" and the passenger complimented him on how good it was, "*perfecto*."

"I never went to Spanish class. I learnt from movies and while drunk talking to other Spaniards." Clem bids him farewell and drives away.

"Lies, complete lies. Why am I still carrying this baggage?"

"Oneupmanship, all the way!" Clem had recently done a course in Spanish, it had improved him a little and he'd also bought a Learn Spanish CD in March. Why did he have to go further? Why did he have to manifest himself into something he is not? Why?

He reasoned that he was still not comfortable in himself. There is still something missing. Mariella had responded to a recent post on his Facebook status "honourable mention: Christopher Hitchens, R.I.P. 'learn not what to think but how to think.'" Mariella posted her graduation photo with her father. She really is a beautiful woman.

The two had their own language.

Between the journey of Dante to the dark side and hanging on to the social norm, there was only always going to be one winner. Clem felt that he had probably already crossed the line. The line that this overbearing question would again and again be revisited as Dante warned. Clem believed that he had the ability to return to a normal life once he crossed the mountain of darkness. He hated the baggage that restricted him. Abstract, not clinical, yet.

He had a writer, previously published, in the taxi. Partially blind, ugly man. Forty-three years old, who looked ten years older. A decent kind man. He conceded that Clem's work was better. Clem told him of what he was planning to do. The writer told him, "The mind is a dangerous place to go alone."

"Thanks for the advice, I go there with full and conscious consent," Clem replied.

Another deadline had passed, Clem had not yet had his poems published and it was now a full two months since the invite to read at the university. He was up to sixty poems, half of which were 'work', half of the remainder bad art, fifteen or so were very good.

January 21st was his next deadline. It is hard for him to ignore the rewards that come with success. He had felt it, seen it. It is strange, how when he told someone he was a writer, how they clicked in a little more. If between them they had time he would show a few poems. Some would feign interest, as many, understanding, then of the others, a few really liked them.

He was after doing more research. Today, he had come to the conclusion that, though he believed in evolution and was near on an atheist, an atheist must accept that it will remain unprovable for the foreseeable future.

It is logical to accept that the 'God' argument has a tenuous argument. Under the domain of specific doctrines, scriptures, rhetoric and here-say it is easily exposed. These have been valuable in some circumstances to the advancement of civilisation. The crimes they perpetrated however? Are they validated by the laws and culture that governed at the time? Or was it plain wrong?

The consequences of a God. An insurance policy. We will all meet again one day, is one of the hardest to conceptualise to any logically minded human functioning brain. It is a beautiful idea but has more of a feel of the cliché 'the grass is always greener on the other side.' This for most 'atheists' is the problem with the human species.

It is not to determine that we are not an optimistic bunch. That we cannot appreciate the marvel of human endeavour or achievement, the sparkling brilliance to set against the mundane or mediocre or indeed the mastery of beauty in its simplicity. This is what we yield to, to enjoy in life.

Why a colour? Why it catches us, stirs us? Why a particular shade? All the equations set forth from the beginning of the universe, to bring a particular moment, place, the variables, the mysterious, subtle and overpowering to our human senses.

The interactions with people. The simple conversations, complex interactions, implied meanings, hidden agendas, complete empathy and total lack of understanding of another's point of view. We are not immoral.

Clem discovers Ayn Rand. Her hypothesis that reality exists independent of consciousness, that humans have direct contact with reality through sense of perception, that one can attain objective knowledge through the process of concept formation and inductive logic, that the proper moral purpose of one's life is the pursuit of one's own happiness! Or rational self-interest, that the only social system consistent morality is full respect for individual rights embodied in 'laissez faire' capitalism, and that the role of art in human life is to transform humans' metaphysical ideas by selective reproduction of reality into a physical form—a work of art—that one can comprehend and to which one can respond emotionally.

> "My philosophy, in essence, is
> the concept of a man as a
> heroic being, with his own
> happiness as the moral
> purpose of his life, with
> productive achievement as his
> noblest activity, and reason
> as his only absolute."

Clem considered the philosophy for a while. He wasn't too confused and understood the rational of it. During the research he wanted to remind himself to check on the U.N. charter for civil rights. Clem giggled inside upon further research into Rand, how many peers, would describe her arguments for Objectivist ethics as fallacious. There was going to be a lot of that in philosophy.

A seed would set in. Set into his mind later on. It would be nice or good to have 'nice things' around. Things that wouldn't possess. Clem wasn't talking in the realms of fantasy this time.

He was a bit of an accidental hoarder, more by the fact he never tidied up, than to holding on to sentimental things, that seemed sentimental, *'well, sentiment usually perished before the material.'*

It had been a long time since Clem had looked in his biscuit tin of letters. The house had got a few makeovers. And sometimes when looking for something else in a drawer, he'd remember similarly looking for those letters. His lower arm, hands reaching out for another letter to find underneath the bag or envelope that held them all together.

These days, he was as happy as being in a place where the thought would come to him, he'd pause, breathe deeply and inhale the memories, turn away, it would fill his mind for a while.

He liked having things, his guitar, he didn't find it particularly attractive. It was a seventies mass manufactured type. Very standard. With the guitar, the value wasn't really in the way it looked, for he'd fallen for many an item that looked 'too good to be true' only for its real value to materialise once he got his hands on it.

He liked, on occasion, dressing sharp. A good suit, toned body, good shoes, cash in his pocket. For a while it felt powerful but it wouldn't last too long. He'd thought briefly of the money he'd saved, not a fortune, before asking briefly, *'what was the use of it?' 'The bar in Spain… oh yeah,'* he imagined it, it was cool. It was good to be putting the money away for it. There was merit in it.

Madrid was now the desire, the bar. The love of something real. Vaguely real, so vague, it was nearly fictitious. The desires would die down, something else would come along and he'd jump for that, it only started to dawn on him. He'd been jumping from one thing to the next thing all his life.

When he was relaxed he was able to go along with the mainstream quite easy, something would catch his eye and he was off, a hundred miles an hour, not always on the outside.

But just in his mind, now, with the poetry book deadline on the horizon he was keeping his cards close to his chest. He'd be really glad to make it to Madrid and stop thinking deeply about subjects, he would be glad to 'just be' with a little curiosity again. He needed to stop being in perpetual motion, in his mind anyway. A break from the constant 'whys?'.

It may be no use just sitting there but it's nice to have it around when you need or want it.

Chapter 11

Am I the Devil Incarnate?

Christmas, how does Clem view Christmas?

He is torn. He will get a little nostalgic come Christmas eve. To the animals, planets, of the northern hemisphere it is just another day in winter. To Clem it is a tug between his beliefs and compromise. He is compassionate. This compassion has a cost unto himself. In a karmic way he believes that he is at power by certain reactions to send forth positives forces into the world.

Placating equations, for the sake of it, send those around him home a little better. Who hence forth from that equation might send forth other equations that might come back to him down the line. If they do not come back to him, then, that they might arrive at someone else's feet is fine by him. But generally it's a bit of lip service. It has lessened in value to little more than a summer barbecue. The pretending is big. Another year around the sun. 'Fairytale of New York', the best bit of which, is the argument.

If the seven billion people on this planet set out to do good, then good, is the most probable outcome. 'What is good?' It may be asked.

More money came, a bit more went out. He was just tired of it now. He wasn't in the mood for it. He wasn't in the mood for anything, especially remembering. He'd given up remembering. He wasn't the remembering type. Growing up he'd thought so much was about remembering. He hadn't remembered for years. What good was it? Until recently, and the good that it was doing him?

That's why he liked writing, creating, a living remembering. Dead remembering is just a waste. Looking at clocks, at watches. 'Yeah, it was fun, it was great but remember out!!' Alcohol used to enhance his memory. Grass, not so much, that just expands his mind, more equivalent to a sober high, when he didn't get a whitie. That's why gambling took to him. The last race was the last race, up and on with the next one. Of course until you'd no money left. Back to empty pockets. Soles so worn on shoes that the socks were thicker. Pants so braided that the cloth of the underwear was like a rug.

There was a price to it, at the close of doors, close of business. It didn't mean he didn't notice the sky less or the wet concrete footpaths fall under his feet. The sense of warmth on entering the car from the cold windy street. The fact that you'd forgotten to eat. It had been a long, long time since Clem had left with nothing. His bottom line was higher. He left enough for food, bills, generally.

The gaps between gambling had grown over the last while. Weeks, months had passed over time since gambling stints. Where was he heading if he stopped? That route, that God forsaken route. He was going to end up dead at some stage, Jesus, he didn't want the highlight of his day to be a read off the daily newspaper or the years highlight 'what colour are we going to paint the ceiling?' not that.

'At least live!' If he could live for a period he could accept that, consider that. But he'd spent a lot of time sticking his wet finger in the air checking for conditions. He'd sell the end part. *'Just live...live once.'*

He'd won a few battles this year though, no Christmas cards, no tree, no lights or fake snow. He'd hand over the cash to the nephews and nieces and a few side gifts. Three dolls. No Christmas in his house though, not this year, no need. He didn't go for it. Last year, the tree had made it up on Christmas eve, at that, just a bare tree, nothing else. It didn't come down until just before Easter, when Kate would come. The year before it was up two days earlier, with decorations and stood in the room again until a week before Easter.

It wasn't Clem, it was trivial, fuel to the system. The perpetuating never ending system. He understood the system was corrupt but he also knew it wasn't broken. It's not the capitalist, communist or socialist system, just the system of life. That's the one true system that works.

The family would meet on Christmas eve in a bar and he'd promised himself, 'this time next year,' he was fed up of those promises. He was fed of saying the same things in the same spots and nothing was different except he was a year older. He'd hope back then. Hope more than reason. This was the first time he'd more reason than hope. He didn't want to pump up hope. Just get the job done. That's all Christmas was about this year. Just get it done.

Everyday was unimportant. That's the way he had to view it, coldly. As the weeks passed it seemed everything was a Monday or a Friday or nearly one of them. They were his reference points. Start of the week, start of the weekend. They were fading a little. The brainwashing from the late summer and Autumn had set in. His subconscious took over, he was on autopilot, trance-like, dazed, he'd wake himself up in July or around then. He'd stay distant. Distant from himself, from the rest, he'd grown distant over the last year or two. As much by nature, the current economy and its effect on his siblings, friends and the community and as of his own choice.

He'd seen this economic meltdown coming. He'd seen it brew, prepared for it. This was the one that was going to make him. In 2007. It was over and a gargantuan beautiful complex had been built in the city centre. He got a call there on the launch night.

A real estate agent. Mid-forties.

"Where are you off to?"

Wherever.

"Great value at three hundred and seventy five thousand euros, aren't they!" she stated.

"Hmmm!" Clem agreed, whilst really thinking to himself, *'what is going on in this poor deluded souls head!!'*

It was like a doctor telling a patient, "I've solved your problem, you're dead!!"

Nothing had moved in six months. He'd seen that look before. That belief in the eyes. It was in common with priests or the Muslims he'd seen. That blind faith, that no-doubt syndrome, Christ, Clem had had it, or did he? How much at any one particular time? Had he seen, that day, in the bookies, as the man looked at Clem, in that way. Clem knew he was in a weird mental state. It didn't matter what he was gambling on or how much it was, he was just being part of the process.

The look told him, it was happening to him, right there, right then. Someone was looking at him. He responded in his mind, *'it's okay, you're just doing this, there's no more.'* He recognised the look. Clem had seen it, probably given it. It was on him. People get into states of mind all the time. He'd seen them everywhere, it's a process. It's not an addiction, up for conjecture, it's a process that the individual is able to function at, in a perceived domain, at any given moment. It's not an addiction, it's a conscious delusionary choice.

For Clem though, he'd only have to think it, to see it. It was time to stop the process. He'd been waiting for the twenty-seventh to stop. Symbolism again. What was the point of that anymore? Symbolism of walking out a door with the photo of a girl, saying, "okay, from now on… I'm heading to you." Clem finds little to argue. He's accepting of himself, he has little defence. There was no harm perpetuated, he feels there may be something awry about him, something a bit weird. That look was the signal, it was time to stop, time to start. He was glad in a way he was now examining himself.

There must be something in it. In order to make a call on others he'd have to make a call on himself. He knew he'd pulled fast ones, 'fucked people over' and because he did it and it happened to him, didn't mean it was okay to wash over it casually.

Clem started another evening's work. He was edgy, darkly. 'How tragic and weary he'd become.'

Divorced from society with a nervy sense of underlying panic about the stream of conscience thought he'd unveiled. He knew he had entered Dante's inferno. Clem had no God to cling to now. This is the dark forest. Was he going to make it through? He felt naked, exposed, raw, weak. The memories of his tricks piling up against the reservoir of his mind. They'd been buried, hidden, gotten over, did he really have to do this? How far? Why? Couldn't he just have a normal mid-life crisis!

He remembered being taught a lesson in school one day, that, "if you see God you will die." *'I'm not going off blaming everyone,'* he thought.

He was on his way to the shop for his mother that evening, late October early November, it was dark. At the bend of his estate he was petrified that God was around,

‘God was everywhere!’ “Are you God?” He turned to look quickly to the corner of a neighbour’s gate. He turned away quickly. He turned again, “Are you God?” Clem asked. He thought or hoped to see a burning bush, he would be okay. He would be ‘a Moses’. He was petrified of seeing God. His eyes glazed over with worry and the sudden turns.

He’d made the decision for better or for worse. He felt it could kill him. These wanderings inside his mind. It felt like he was in labour, preparing for childbirth or stoned or drunk or all three. Would he still be able to be normal after this? Would he function okay? Like the time he’d given up smoking for eight months and spewed up a mucous, that had spooled itself into a thread or a deep root in a garden. You could pull it, and the more you’d pull of it, the more you’d get, but you’d never get all of it and it would snap, the tail recoiling back deep, to where it would escape his clutch.

An exorcism. Did he really need this? He wasn’t really puritanical. He wasn’t chasing salvation or enlightenment. He thought for a second, consciously interrupting his stream of thought. At times he did want it, at times he could feel it, sense it, whatever that mystery was.

Clem remembered a Sunday, he was about twelve. The journey to the church was short. They were always a little late, less to endure. On the occasions they were early his mindset would be between ‘look at us we are early’ and ‘I wish this started so it would be over’. His father was immaculately dressed as usual. The four, his sister and mother all linked hands. His father was smoking a cigarette, the sun shone bright into Clem’s eyes, he had to squint.

Then, his father threw his half smoked cigarette to the ground and said, “I’m going for a pint!” Clem made the quick calculation, *‘a happy dad, a bit of endurance of drunk love, handshaking, singing and maybe money.’* He’d made that calculation so often before, it was easy but something was different today. He was going. Yes, to the same places, but away from something, he’d made his mind up on something. Something Clem would make his mind up about someday.

He didn’t really like churches, they were too big. Outside and inside. He didn’t mind the stained glass, he just read the words and jumbled them up sometimes to make new ones. He looked around to see what time it was to kneel, to stand and sit down again. Sometimes it was confusing, especially at one point just after the middle of the mass, where it seemed okay to kneel forward at two different times. If you got it wrong and went with the first wave you couldn’t go back and sit, you just had to endure the longer kneel. Sometimes he’d listen to the priest.

He’d understand a bit, for a while, and then his mind would head off. It was always a case of just being there, getting it over, nothing fun, nothing dreary. He’d hang around cold carparks with his younger sister making up games as his mother chatted with neighbours and friends. The playing never took to them. It wasn’t a full-on ‘play place’ you had to hold back. The clothes were too clean.

He knew from that day, one day, he wouldn’t go again, to the church. He’d still be a catholic, he’d still belong to God, he’d still go with his mother and his sister. He was still a boy, child. He realised what his father did that day was ‘a man thing!!’, ‘a really, really man thing!!’ Clem was proud of his father that day.

Was he the devil? He suggested to himself. Was he becoming a mind manipulator? His own mind? Other minds? What buttons was he pressing? Was he becoming the guardian of hell? 'Line them up, lure them in,' who had he followed there? Why could he let his mind go to terrible places, if he wanted to? Was he dark? Really dark? Charm them, let them lose their layers of protection, just let them set their guard down and lure them into his web. Not many victims. But some hung on his word.

Did he just want to drift into the dark? It felt like the universe was coming closer, in the back of his mind, eavesdropping, 'What's he going to say? What's he going to find out? Is the game up?' Like opening this porthole domain of everything was giving him power because he'd not gone mad. He'd still a big strong rope to the real world, when it was time to go back he'd go back.

Why did he feel like the devil now? Had he suckered Mariella in? Played a character, like in the movies, had he only been playing all along? How could he be cured? How after all the relationships could he be cured, fixed again, unaffected. If he didn't want their ass, what had he been chasing? Their minds? Their hearts? Was all that just prep work for taking on God? Play a character, and slide in under sheep's clothing. Who questions it this much? Without going crazy.

It felt at times that part of his mind was getting groggy, black spots, that every thought needed another push or a temporary pause, pretending to walk away before running back and having another push? Was this depression? Was he just depressed? From the outside it could of course look like it. From his vestige he was just hiding. He'd admit, if one wanted to put it down as depression, they could have it.

He'd promised himself. The one ultimate promise, he'd never get depressed and even as a test, he started to pull against himself, for a few seconds, to prove it and he could feel himself summoning that vital energy, that spare vital energy he'd syphoned off for at any time to resort to, to come to him.

So was it a mask? Was he 'in character'? *'Better to lay in the grass a little while longer. Let's pretend I'm depressed. Let's play the Devil Incarnate!!'* Not that he still didn't get spooked or feel an eeriness, just he knew different, somewhere he knew different. He'd never thought of suicide, not an inch. Taunted death a few times but a drunken taunt. In cars, fights, mischief.

In school, about fourteen, the teacher asked a question. "What gifts does a man with no arms, no legs, no sight, speech or hearing have?" Clem knew straight away. He was innocent then, or was he? Did he know more from his mother's episodes than any of them would figure out in a lifetime? He was slightly embarrassed to know? As the teacher went through the twenty-five silent answers before he got to Clem, "you?" "you?" "you?" "… Love!!" Clem answered. It was one of those where fun wasn't made of anyone in the class.

A tingle ran down his back and the hairs stood at the back of his neck. Clem was happy but underneath he already knew there was far more to life than love. In his twenties he came to the conclusion that love, the 'mills and boon' version, was merely a surrender of independence. A back door to avoiding 'oneself'.

So while those around built from the ground up, Clem had set about jumping to the moon and that's all others around could see, a man jumping up and down. 'He was depressed… Really?' Is it as mad to be jumping up to moon as to be putting a couple of bricks together? Clem was a bit of thief, a sneak, he'd steal an odd brick, rarely out of mHelen much more out of necessity.

People climb mountains, it's their goal in life. Clem wanted to climb mountains so it was a closer spot to jump to the moon but here's the devil bit. Was it that he really wanted to jump to the moon and have them believe it... so he could sit back and watch all these people jumping up and down. The thing is, Clem figured, he'd followed someone else in, or been tricked in, but he knew it now. Shouldn't he tell the people who are jumping up and down at the moon? "Look... there's no way you'll ever get there by jumping." But what else was there to do? Build a wall?

With his body married to the car and his mind in a battle with God, the other half of his heart in San Francisco, "I left my heart..." his conscience interjected immediately, *'shut up, Clem!!'* He'd nothing else to do really, except wait.

Chapter 12

Luck!

Luck of the soldier who charged over the trenches in World War one or up the beaches of Normandy in World War two. Which bullets struck which victims? Was it down to what the machine gunner ate for breakfast? Was every event in his life going to lead the gunner to here, at this time?

As for the victim, whose fate rests in the gunner's finger, from his perspective was it a number he picked, at which point did he not speak when he should have or did he speak when he shouldn't?

How he ended in a particular column on a particular day, was it down to the simplicity of a surname in a draft? With such volume there are many variables. Some which take you out of the loop and others that drag you back in.

A customer.

'At last!' Clem thought.

She's an accountant, a non-glorifying job she admits before Clem even asks.

"But it's over and I'm free for Christmas."

She's about thirty-three or thirty-four. Two children at home. She can't wait to get back and sleep, wake up tomorrow and spend time with them over the holidays.

Clem is grateful for her presence. Unlike his own mother, she has a career. It could be better, it could be worse, going back to his sister's holistic theory.

Turning atheist is a lonely jump. It is foolish to think you can do without people.

The lady in the taxi talks of things in the Ukraine. They sing a song between them for half the journey. Clem doesn't know much about the Ukraine. Kiev, which he mentions. Chernobyl, which he doesn't, gladly later because he remembers that it is in Belarus. And he forgot the name of the 'Orange revolution' which he finds funny because that's what it was called, he thinks. He'd never have got Yushchenko's name right either.

They were able to discuss on an even field. She was after a few 'break up from work drinks'. No religion was discussed. He'd asked her what she'd really like to do? Between the fantasy of the ballet and the love of her kids, advancing up the ladder of accountancy her main wish. Clem thought fleetingly about when she was fifty and her kids were grown. Like his own mother, how would she deal with that.

This woman had a career though, which might safeguard her. Clem did compare his own 'marvellous existence' honestly. As of now he was socially excluded. A taxi driver. Single and physically weak. His choice of deviating from the crowd had a coldness to it. Not everyone was crossing over or openly doing so. Though the knowledge was there, people were still holding back.

Maybe a reaction to struggling economies, the pattern was spreading quicker in the younger generation, they having more time to gamble with.

Was Clem now immersed in Dante's inferno? At least others had crossed over. It's easy to say it. One's an 'atheist'. It's harder to believe it, but acting upon it required from him a little more fortitude.

More customers. Choosing between the black driver in front and the guy writing in a copy book. Clem needed money for his Spanish lifestyle. Tonight, he needed distraction more because this contemplation was exhausting.

With the symbols of getting into character, coffee drinking, chain smoking, chocolate and fast-food eating, unclean, unshaven, anti-system, mild self-doubting, unkempt melancholic mind, he'd reached the line.

As he queued another few minutes he knew earlier he'd visited the line. The line that the conscience holds onto. It has to decide to come in and intervene and draw oneself away from it.

A customer, a student, drunk.

Clem is buoyed. The passenger sends and receives a few text messages.

"How's life?" Clem asks.

"Just finished exams!"

"Assassination I?"

"Huh?"

"It's a joke,"

"Nah, it was a hangover test from last Wednesday… nothing worse," the student continues

"Leprosy on your balls, I'd reckon!!" Clem interrupts "I know... it's a bitch waiting like that."

"So, what are you studying?" Clem continued.

"Culinary arts."

"Is there a lot of art in that?" Clem asks in a curious tone.

"There's a bit of art in it," the student replies.

"There's cooking and cooking, I guess. I mean, it's still food. And yeah, some people are going to be better at it than others, some so good they turn it into an art along the way, right?"

"Yeah, that's about it," Clem agreed digesting the information.

"Do you watch Masterchef?" Clem asks.

"I watch the Irish one, not the Australian one…" the student responds.

"I think it's hilarious…" Clem puts on an accent "Oh, what you haven't done to those mushrooms. And the salmon, the fillet is amazing, with the herbs and the flavours and the colours," Clem changes accent again, "and the music in the background… dah, dah, dah, we're all going to dieee!!"

The passenger laughs a little.

"So did you ever slay an animal?" Clem asks.

"Yeah, just a chicken. It's not nice."

"Yeah," Clem agrees. "It makes you appreciate where meat comes from. Not just having forty-seven burgers in a barbecue and chuffing them down."

The student is off to the States, he has 'connections out there'.

Clem had an opportunity, like that once, he's glad he never took it.

Clem gets a job at the base. A neighbour. They have a laugh on the journey. Helen is next, 'another woman who rules the world'. Clem is angry, he is waiting and in the meantime got another call from a regular, which would fit in kindly to this fare. 'Very nice mind you but tentacles that reach and repress those that are around. Control problems, we all have those I suppose'. Clem starts to write more forgivingly. If she did enter the taxi upon him writing and found these words she'd have war.

Clem gets the other job done rapidly enough. He's back in the rank, the queue is rolling handy. Christmas nights out, one-fifteen a.m. and Clem is living again. It is a relief, a quick look at Mariella's profile, she's added two friends and he closes the link.

Back to mainstream.

It sometimes, takes something else, a different equation, force, to engage with a 'sitting' dormant being. It creates a 'flow', a catalyst. It causes an exponential force unto it, 'the human' runs into 'a space' where the equations interacting with it, 'the human', become limited, less and less, and it, 'the human', starts to retract in decreasing circles until again it meets a catalyst. It 'the human', is also a catalyst but without other elements it is dormant.

External equations are derived from many things. Population density, occupation, current lifestyle.

Many, many ponderables, that are so many they seem imponderable. Clem is back to the top of the queue. He is less fearful of going back to the 'inferno' of his mind. He has wondered before if this is the secret?

The night passes on smoothly. A conversation with a customer gives him encouragement. Clem compares to him that now in humanity, a humanity without God, is like living after our parents have died. That 'WE' are responsible now, for the world, as best we can tender to it. It should not daunt us. The passenger, listening intently, is impressed by Clem's take on things.

It happens that he is a practising psychiatrist. Clem asks him one question, he's wanted to ask for a long time, "Is any one person, unsalvageable?" the psychiatrist answers. "No, it's just a matter of time and resources!"

Clem returns to the evolution theory. His questioning now, are we here, by 'God' or 'evolution' or a 'third' as of yet unknown way. So, if in time we do not need the Earth, is it therefore logical that if there was 'a God', 'Big Bang' or 'Third way' whether indeed any of the three are needed anymore.

Like cycling, does one need to consciously remember all the techniques involved in cycling every time they get on a bike? Maybe, if there is a God, it might be in the past tense, maybe there was 'a God'? He just gave us a push and for one day, like life we don't need a dependency on that God anymore. What was that God? Was it the Big Bang? Was it indeed a deity who's act was indeed to sacrifice him, her, itself for us. Is that the thing we carry? Or is there another force?

With some of the weaknesses in arguments being opened on the internet, the truth could be harder to figure with so many vested interest groups, relating to evolution. Did indeed, things, just happen that way? for no particular reason, it just happened without any interest at all. This obviously resonates more to the Big Bang. There was no issue, motive, involved with the Big Bang, just an occurrence. Is that what we are? Just an occurrence? 'Probably… just here for the duration,' seems believable. 'Just a piece of energy?'

What does that lead us to? Well if the species runs from 'A to B', parallel with our perceived time, then outside of that nothing matters. For individuals, we know when 'A' starts, as a whole, it could be argued we were fractions before that but as a whole being we do not begin, until we suck our first bit of air, we might be living as foetus, we'll call it twenty-four weeks after conception, it's generally too late for a termination after that, let others get into that ethical debate.

Everyone who has died has gone from 'A to B'. Those that are dead are at 'B'. Those yet to be born are somewhere before 'A'. That leaves the rest of us between 'A and B'. 'A to B' happens for everyone, so far, anyway. So what's that about? What are we meant to do between 'A and B'? "Life is a slither of light between two dark places," a writer once wrote. *'It's strange then that so many dark places can be found during that light!!'*

"We need more light!!" Clem exclaims. "The darkness of life has its attractions but we need more light!!"

He ponders, the advancement of humanity. It's working. Through endeavour of previous generations our world is brighter now, individuals freer, freer minds means a less frustrated, fearful being. The current news being circulated in the media about poor economic hardships for the coming years or decades is a fearmongering, doomsday propaganda that has dogged humanity throughout its existence. It follows individuals through their lives. It is a burden, a carrier of darkness, an enemy of the human mind. Problems that are not insolvable, manipulated to sell fear to the masses.

Clem recognises governance. Is there really a one percent? Do the one per cent know they are in the one per cent? There is obviously a one per cent of the poorest people in the world too. Why isn't there a protest about that. Surely their need is a lot more dire than the need of the protesting centre, who must surely average out at a range above the fifty per cent mark?

Organisations that do look after the one percent of the poorest people have developed their own market strategies. Selling conscience, peace of mind to those who donate. Clem is not against it. Like the reluctant social service worker, once it gets done. What is happening in the world though? Why the same problems? Are the problems the same? Get a job, get married. Clem is proud of the younger generation. A lot of them want to see the world, experience life more on a spiritual level. They haven't given up on older notions of meeting 'prince charming' or 'sleeping beauty', they just want to see things, feel things, taste things.

This was a curse of a night, a waiting night. Midnight would be a relief, at least the calendar would click over once more. One number closer. He could sense that nagging back, not far away. *'Go home,' 'you're tired,' 'you deserve it.'* "Go away!" he'd shout. *'Look at what you've done already,'* he'd glimpse and pertinently turn away in his mind. "You're not getting to me!" rather than having to wait and listen to himself, the next best thing was to drive. "Don't you listen to him!!" he ordered himself. He knew the queue was moving. Moving quickly. It was Christmas, people were about. Hang on, he'd turn the volume up on the radio.

He hated Facebook now. Mariella had been making moves back towards him. Status updates that were deliberately for him. She'd known coming up to her birthday that he could use it as the ultimate weapon. Would he be cruel or forgiving? On his birthday in April she stuck a knife in him. She was vicious. She never sent him a message. Just a status update the following day about 'counting double if you throw someone off a mountain'.

She started a website about him, the following day. Clem laughed and found it quite complimentary. Her birthday had been oncoming and she realised how much she missed him, liked him. Clem knew if he was mean now, it would destroy everything. He wanted to still give it a chance. After September, when she'd done him, he started getting into philosophy on a grander scale. It annoyed the hell out of her that after all the begging over two days he could just stop, get back to living and what was worse he was into something.

As bad as it is seeing a guy chase another girl, it's worse when they're into something bigger than all that. It was as much pretence as real. Coinciding with the God question taking him away from the love question. It fitted so well. He'd some unfinished poems and in the space of a week he'd another fifteen. Better, just better, as good as the ones back in April but about so much more than love.

He'd one saved, again using her as his muse. He sent it and she responded positively. She'd given him the cue to return the revenge she'd applied to him, but he didn't. Now, back in the car, it was a case of waiting until she got fed up again or angry. The distance thing was ridiculous.

Every time he clicked on her profile he was waiting for her to be a bitch. He'd no cards. He was still way behind in the game of everything! What had he to offer? A million to one chance. People wake up and don't buy that. It was going to happen one day. One day it would all be over. Once Clem got closer and closer to August, the compensation would be physical. He was lost.

'What was it about him?' she thought to herself. Even now. This far away. He'd still a grip. He'd made an idiot out of her, even though she destroyed him over and over again. Did she really have this much power over him? Over men. Once they didn't see it, too quickly. They were all chasing her, those that bit. He'd swallowed whole and got nothing. His poems were too good to come from a dumb man, an idiot perhaps.

Was he that lacking in confidence? Didn't seem to, but he drunk. Still, he hadn't that excited boyish panicking enthusiasm that accompanies it. He was older though! A little more experienced. *'Why didn't he dive in when I opened the door? He'd seen them, hadn't he?'*

She pouted, she knew, they were in the photos and he looked, bumbling idiot. Mariella combed her hair. It was her shield, it was her weapon. It covered her great blemish. She'd kinda grown fond of them, she liked them. They were a test, to the shallowness of a man. They were all shallow and if they weren't shallow they were boring or plain.

'All the guys, better looking guys, Jose, Carlos, Mau, why him? Always looking in and why do I like it? And why do I look back? And why do I get such a rage when I see him doing anything else. Talented man!! huh idiot.'

San Francisco was being kind to Mariella. She was over Javi and escaped the near disaster with Alberto, Clem hadn't found out. It didn't matter now, he was gone, out of the picture. *'Who am I kidding?'* she thought to herself. *'No, I am!'* she reaffirmed. Who else on Facebook could she communicate without being on her 'friends list, she thought.

Dani had come and gone. Sergi, well, he just isn't biting. *'What do they think I am? a washing machine for cocks?'*

Mariella was missing home. It was like Coventry. Away from home but again surrounded by Spanish speakers, at least this time she wasn't with Pedro. Clem had done for him. They were done anyway. And Jose had done Clem. Finally, the end of him and she again looking for Clemency. She gave him that! She found herself begging, well pleading, for another chance how did he manage that? Mariella had given him the run around so, so often. Enough of him.

She was a great adventurer but this was the first time on her own and people after a few months of openness, started retreating towards their shell. They didn't belong here, she'd known already nothing was going to change romantically. The man of her dreams wasn't here, and if he was, he just belonged more in someone else's dream, like Sergi.

She loved computers, she loved everything, she got so fed up. She hated so much. When would everything be hers? She was getting older. Twenty-four. Nothing, no boyfriend. She was glad in a way. No suffocating, no questions, no worrying about him, it was nice to be free, she wasn't giving that back.

She'd found a power in herself, her hair, a confidence. She could hypnotise with it, her mind could manipulate men through it. She'd developed a strong image. A confident image. 'The girl next door was leaving her'. '*Ahhh*!' She still didn't know what she wanted. She wanted a chance to live ten lives simultaneously but only ever had room for one and in truth there was a whole lot voids in that. Spaces. For all the hype and California was truly great, there were classes, there was work, there was a little of the 'sameness' developing, there was thinking.

She'd only arrived and having tested the water, she was already feeling out a tentacle for home. Especially late November, December. Home got on without her. She wasn't really needed. The gap temporarily filled. She was alone, like they all were. Unlike those that found love. It hadn't found her, here, yet, but there's always a door opening.

Clem was nearly shaking. He was heading to diabetes or OPCD or something. He needed to stop, it was directly manifesting itself physically now. The springboard would happen. He went home and checked his poems. Seventy-five!! How many did he need? For a book, a collection. He sort of guessed he might have crossed a finishing line. But did he have enough? Tim, a guy who he collected drunk or stoned or both, had been a writer. Tim was a year ahead in school and Clem would show him a few poems.

Tim was into the Dalai Lama and had pilgrimaged over to him "something else," Tim wasn't a hippie but had a kind, honest, solid heart whom Clem had always liked. Once he arrived in Tibet with £3,000 spending money and on seeing the poverty just handed over the cash.

You've got to do something with those poems, he said. "Twenty or thirty," was the count according to Tim. A girl from the university, an English professor, was also impressed. "Come in to the English lit. society" Clem was against that in theory. Mainly because he didn't feel he had the volume for it. He never really felt he'd enough until he was pushed. Clem gave of his all when writing, most times anyway. After that it was like he'd never written them at all. He'd read them, forget that he wrote them.

He'd do the book. The book of poems, definitely. His friend encouraged him to just get something done. Just get something down. He'd do it. January 10th. He didn't figure anything on it but it was strange, would he still be himself after this? After all the 'I'm gonnas' that never came to fruition, a week later he was warned, "you're going to have to learn to humility!"

'What? I'm always humble!!' he thought. *'Why are you so defensive?'* he swiftly jumped across himself in his mind. That's something he could agree with, it had been years now since he'd been told. He could hear himself so often being defensive. He hadn't heard it in a while though because he had been spouting a self-justification monologue for the longest time now. He was starting to look forward to thinking about God again, *'all his*

fault,' he chuckled to himself. Before quickly realising the darker side of him was still not far out of focus. Wasn't this what the whole thing is about?

Chapter 13

Clem is ill now. Really ill. He feels the tingles more, around and through his body. He knows he is exhausted. He is intaking too much sugar and lack of exercise is going to be severely detrimental to his health. He's half convinced his hypochondria has some merit, lying in bed he feels the calf of his legs reverberate. The pain isn't a great one. It's a scary one. His heart is giving a little jolt now and again too. Not that big, is it a murmur? Is it Mariella? Is it Kate? There is definitely some stress correlation. Ignorance of many things, guidelines freely available have come to him and been ignored, now, he concludes that it is time to change, in February.

He passes another symbolic date, the winter solstice with the promise of change. It passes, he hasn't changed. At least he can stop looking at the top of the milk bottle and its best before date as a reference point. He never remembers how that crept in, but it did and it didn't stop. He must take responsibility for his physical wellbeing. He must now take responsibility for himself.

His cough cannot be blindly ignored. His infatuation with the internet and all it encompasses must be toned down. The stock market, Mariella and the YouTubing must be reduced. It only leads to stress which he feels is mentally compounded all over the infrastructure of his body. He must govern properly the domain of his own body and mind.

Clem has been gamble-free, let's rephrase that, casino-free for five months now. He feels he is 'cured'. He has no want of it anymore. Clem took up golfing again, two years ago, having play intermittently since a teenager. A little group formed together, a competitive group. They were escaping. It seemed it was the only important thing in the world for a period. Who would get the lowest score? In such events, prove their worthiness to the world.

Clem knew what this was about. The world didn't care. It might have spread as far as twenty people at a push but to them for a period it was everything. They knew it was idiocy, it was just a part of them that needed to escape the reality or perceived reality of things for a while. It happened with Terence before. With a band and PlayStation.

The band was formed in 1998. They managed to fill a few practice rooms. Had twenty minutes of success where they sounded really, really good, people know when these things happen, it's just that the audience is thin. They never managed to get further due to two things. Musical differences and a lack of will. Who knows what they could have achieved but they were doomed forever to nothing, except that twenty minutes, because of a lack of will.

No one would have ever found what they achieved on PlayStation. They played on and off for three to four years between their late twenties and early thirties. Here presented itself a world in disguise of the world that they couldn't control or 'succeed in'. It was addictive. It's why they got on so well. Subconsciously and sometimes consciously they weren't happy with things in their lives.

Clem had put that to bed quickly. He'd been driving home and thought he 'really didn't like golf,' if he could apply the same discipline to the guitar wouldn't he be better for it. There was a guitar around the house, lying next to his father's dusty slippers. It was three and a half years since he'd died. Mariella had passed a comment on a guitarist's profile a few weeks earlier, this grated on him. He'd tried the guitar once before but never got the hang of it. He started again, this time to learn by ear, like the last time.

Kate came home, it was her guitar originally, and bought him a beginner's book. Which Clem started to learn from as soon as she headed back to Italy. Clem hated admitting it but there was a lot of merit to Kate's advice. Didn't he just like hearing it or hearing it from her? Also, how easy had it been for him to take up the guitar from Mariella's comment and the likelihood down the line if he ever got any good at it, deny she had any part to play in it. Clem had some growing up to do, a lot of growing up to do or at least he had some acknowledging to administer.

Clem became proficient, in some way, on the guitar. With his learning from the book and not learning from the book he was able to play a song or two, this would be handy when he'd make his decision to go to Spain, this time, the one for certain time. Following on from this loose logical step, was where he grew the confidence to take on other projects, particularly the work ethic side of things. He was turning capitalist, building bricks. He was building a wall.

Clem and Terry united under a fantasy umbrella, they wished for more, something else, something different. They'd chat and push each other's dreams along. Terry had structure. Terry had a good life. His social life was limited more by the slow progress of his friends in the group than anything else. He was heading to forty, looking pretty. A full head of hair, Clem wouldn't have minded, off cigarettes nearly a year now. *'What is keeping everybody?'* ran through his head. He knew things didn't run the same for all his friends, *'but come on! Patrick up to his eyes in trouble. Clem, Clem still wanting to be in a boy band, or whatever scheme it was now, at least he was working, making alternative plans. Noel was in a dire struggle of his own but Patrick, Patrick , Patrick!!! What was happening to Patrick?'* He was defeated? Possessed by no will?

They'd a falling out early that year. It was an economic reason, revolving around Patrick. Terry was doing really well, one of the few, in the current economic climate. His brother was an astute ballsy businessman who'd cornered the segment of a trading market for a brief period of time.

He'd made millions. He'd done well before, lost it and got rich again. You could say he'd the knack, the luck, the balls, the work ethic. Whatever you put it down to, he had it. Terry was his brother's first disciple. Terry was fine with that, never a begrudging sort, he worked that role very hard and could foresee the benefits he'd reap for himself. He was the perfect wingman for any company, once he believed in it.

Patrick like so many in these times was at the other end of the spectrum. He'd got into business too. The notion is attractive but the work tedious. A handsome man, that had girls swooning as they looked in his green eyes and thick jet-black hair. He was charming, intelligent and quite passive.

Money had been doled out by the banks in the state. He and his business partners had clean financial records and took on personal loans to fund the business. Money dried up everywhere and Patrick like so many others was up the creek.

"Patrick should be working!" was Terry's mantra.

"Why?" Clem would argue.

"He's got a wife and young child to look after!"

"Who knows if that is the best reason for doing something?" Clem defended.

"Huh! I've set him up with some interviews and stuff. Got him a job in a chipper van for £75 a night if he wants it. 'Nah!' he says! You'd do it, wouldn't ya?" Terry ranted

"Depending on the circumstances, yeah," Clem agreed.

"It's like it's beneath him or something!!" Terry griped over the phone.

Fifteen years ago Clem had wanted to earn some extra money. He'd been offered a similar position by his lifelong friend but turned it down. Clem knew if it was between him and dying he'd do it but how far up from that would he still be willing to work. He knew for a lot of his own rhetoric, his actions were a poor gesture. Clem owned up and told Terry.

"Yeah, well I guess if he wants it bad enough he'll do it," Clem declared but he felt it necessary to point out Patrick's 'rights or position' in all of this.

It became personal, it happens when ideologies, even when they seem so similar, clash. The arguing went on for weeks. It was never really personal but attacks on Patrick seemed to be indirect attacks on Clem. Clem didn't like it. He liked the ability to figure it out for himself.

Clem was fine with working, he hated it sometimes, but he would do it. He'd done a lot harder jobs for less and dropped people off every day to work where it was as physically tiring as it was brain numbing. It was a lot better than being stuck in a sewer for ten hours, near Brehamwood. It was better than waiting in a greenhouse until quarter to five to come so he could head away. It was better than answering the same question after question in a call centre. Clem was lucky, he knew that, but he still wanted more. He was fine, only suffering the near insane motionless once or twice a week inside a car with a shitful of useless information going through his mind.

Why was it different for Patrick? Why should he go to a place he didn't want to be, doing a thing he didn't want to do, talking to people he didn't want to talk to? The rewards for him on a personal level didn't match up to what was to be gained. So maybe it was easier for him to hide away and find something that was soothing against the displeasure of not having certain things or pressures exercised from institutions rather than suffer the pain of an endless slog in other areas, just because 'it's a job!'. It fits the mould for so many unworthy occupations of one's time and hence life.

Clem had been to the beach, escaping again, looking for a symbol, looking for something. January 2010. A girl on his mind again, Mariella. Before her, it had been Agneiskwa, before her Marija and before that it was someone else.

A beautiful crisp clear day. He walked around a park next to a little shore. A man was gathering debris of driftwood that had washed up on the shore. Clem at first, assumed it was dry seaweed for the garden, that's what he'd seen people do before.

"Lovely day!!" the man said as he passed by to fill up the little van.

"Beautiful!!" Clem replied after being taken over by his mind, drifting to bright lilac sky. He looked down to a little cove, where he'd been swimming but two months ago at four a.m. in minus-two-degree temperature. *'Do it.' 'just to show you're still alive!!'* He rolled his eyes up at himself mentally.

"This is what life's all about!!" the man continued.

"Seems to be," Clem replied only getting a little instant to think.

"The country's fucked!!" the man said. Clem gave what seemed a knowing look.

"I'd eighteen men working for me three years ago," the man went on. "I'm broke now and I couldn't be happier!!" Clem leaned toward him, he was thinking of joining in, agreeing, but he'd let the man have his say.

"I'm up here gathering this for fire so the kids can have a bath later on," Clem nodded his approvement, he didn't know what else to do. Somewhere on the man's face was a worry and pride, no shame. No shame in his voice.

"Working my balls off, for what? To work some more?"

Clem listened, he was heading toward his hymn sheet but this wasn't his audience, this wasn't his time. "I've never had it better, 'fuck all!' but loads of time."

'Here's a banana!' Clem cruelly thought for a second, it crept in, that vicious 'pull no punches' side of him. He'd been in his mind referring to the true value of a life. 'It ain't all about the money.' He'd accused his father, during a row, that all he was ever interested in was the money. It took Clem aback when he realised it had hurt him. They'd been arguing over what Clem was going to do with his life. Clem was claiming he didn't know what to do and maybe he could be the next 'John Lennon'.

"You're no John Lennon," his father answered.

"Well, John Lennon wouldn't have been John Lennon if he'd have been raised in this house."

He'd regretted that, something about it. He learned from it slowly, started recognising things in his father he'd never seen. Maybe that's where Kate had missed out. They'd seen him being an asshole but because Clem was still around he'd seen him being a man. A different man in different situations but first a man, whatever that composed of, 'taking care of things… maybe badly, but no one's going to reach a hundred per cent.'

"It's nice here," claimed Clem. The man took a look, he'd been taking a look during his industry. "It's great man, it's great!" he answered positively. Clem agreed. The man didn't ask him. Didn't suggest it. He wasn't doing too much blaming. He knew he'd had his chance, his choice to pull back at any stage, when he'd more money than he could count. Drawn in, just drawn in.

After six months of silence, Terry and Clem started reconciling. Enough time had elapsed and it was time to get over things. The first meeting was fine, great, like they were twenty again. Things were strange though. They were both changing, it didn't mean they liked each other any less. Certain subjects were not becoming taboo but just hard to understand, to approach.

It seemed as if an invisible Earthquake was happening in Ireland and people didn't know where it was carrying them. Cracks and crevices formed, the effort needed to cross divides becoming greater and greater. People were looking at each other from further and further away. This, concurring with their perspective ages in life, it would be hard to see the plates meander back to where they once were, if at some stage they drew closer. It was life, people had to do their own thing.

There wasn't enough time or resources to scout too much for others. It was a damning indictment of Irishness. The best thing about them was shown here, they had the honesty with each other to admit it. A draw, Clem could live with a draw. No 'oneupmanship'.

On reflection he would think why God was not so present amongst these friends. Being with them it was like 'God Lite'. He wasn't ever really lurking around that much. It seemed more the presence of ether or sky or laughter was around. Even if the topic amongst the gossip got darker. It took Clem a while to remember why no sense of impending doom seemed to be close by, an ambivalence to the subject.

Chapter 14

The Catastrophic Consequences of Being Untidy

The far-reaching effect and meaninglessness of life can be ascertained by any one individual to the relevant or irrelevant spectre in which that one individual occupies or desires there to. The catastrophic consequences of being untidy is what Clem delves into next.

As revealed earlier Clem can cook but rarely cooks, it's not that hard, follow the process. It's not ergonomic, what he buys to cook is always good food. Special offer or reduced, usually closing in on a 'sell by date'. He hasn't been eating well lately, not with Madrid, not with the thinking, not with Mariella, he'd lost a lot of weight. Brais, a good friend from Vigo, had posted a quote from Buddha, translated as best as:

"Men, will lose health to raise money for restoring their health, worry themselves so much about the future, forget about present living so much that they never achieve either. Live as if they were never going to die, and die as if they never lived."

Clem had been geeing himself up, getting ready for the 'big one', the one jump. He didn't know whether it was aimed at him but he could see the similarities of it and his current mantra. 'Make money,' 'must go to Spain,' 'make money,' 'must go to Spain.' It was late August. Clem had finally got an investment account. He'd finally got the two thousand but first he found out eleven hundred was plenty to open the account. It was the safe haven for gambling money. All future gambling money would go there.

Wanted to gamble? Go to bank, deposit, go to stockbrokers, write cheque, wait. Check account. Your balance is £2,300. It was great, it was gone. No ATM card to withdraw it. Just dump it in there and build and forget about it. Clem had been posting a bit on Facebook about his plans, mainly to convince himself, put the gun to his head, a covert message to Mariella.

The covert messages started at the end of 2009. Facebook was young enough, the explosion hadn't happened. They conversed by messages, Clem sending more. Mariella had a boyfriend. The same one she'd had for about two years now, the same one in Zaragoza, that she'd cared not to mention. Clem had asked.

Clem sent her a poem in November, the first one he'd written in nearly three years. He'd got back to the book he'd been writing that was in a competition with slippers and the guitar for which could stay in the one spot the longest. But her birthday was approaching and Clem was set on writing her a poem. She wrote on her status two days later. It was clearly for Clem.

It kept going, sometimes she'd respond in English, sometimes in Spanish, mostly to his messages, sometimes to his status updates. Clem didn't like that bit of it. She was taking over what he was saying on his own wall. She started adding 'likes' as a response, when things got het up between the two from two thousand and eleven, anytime he confronted her directly in a message, she'd the ultimate defence. It was like she was saying one thing on one level, and meaning something else on another. It was becoming frayed.

He'd been here before. Fantasy disguising a sour reality, he wanted to stop it. The golf, it had nothing at all to with anything. It was PlayStation, the thing that it reminded him of most. Hours and hours of dedication, building up a world, having discussions about it, the only thing on a mind. The pull was huge. He knows that world. He started off years before on Scramble, Pacman, Donkey Kong. He'd save his pocket money and journey into the arcade. The school caught on fire once. It suited him, it had just become his turn and he'd be able to play away in peace.

He'd felt for a while he was the only one. The only one who this affected. This mindset. Everyone else was being normal, getting on with it. Not him, he was worse. It was strange now, how Facebook had seven hundred million members. How, when he'd go to an office in town, there it was on the screen of the lower bar of the secretary's computer.

It affected others differently. If Mariella hadn't been around, he'd have lost interest easy enough but it was the only line of communication between the two. Well, there were two others, but they were last resorts. It was a sign of the times how video games had overtaken DVD sales. What was going on here? Were so many people slipping behind a freely available veil?

It had annoyed Clem, Brais' post, Brais is a gent, and the man has less ill feeling in his bones than nearly anyone Clem knows. He knows Brais knows something, the way Clem knows something. It took Clem two days to come up with a comment, they'd been rolling over in his mind, "Personally… I prefer to show him the light, than another voice who tells him 'he is in the dark'…" he knew the second he pressed 'comment' he'd got it wrong, sounded way too 'Godlike', 'egotistical,' what was he doing at all... sometimes, was he writing *Mein Kampf*?, was he 'number one in the world?'

He trolled around and found a comment line relating to another Buddha saying where the comment read, 'ask the Buddha to be that way when he's working for £5.65 an hour in Tesco.' That summed it up so much better.

People are trying. Clem was trying. He was in full mode and really didn't want to listen to rhetoric that he talked more than anyone. Clem had realised they are great to have as your fundamental core principles but it's nice to find a good place to park your ass.

Clem is untidy, very untidy. He can clean, half reluctantly does so when the time arrives. It is concurrent with whatever situation arises in order for him to keep an element of control in any situation or situation arising. The visit of 'the sister'.

Kate. Kate is a self-made modern-day woman. Heroine or hated? Sometimes both. Extremely controversial and a poor judge of subtlety. Left for England in eighty-four a qualified nurse. Worked in a hospital for a few years, got married and pursued advancement through a math degree. Moved herself and her family to Sydney for seven years, where she picked up a masters in Geology. And on to Brest, when her second marriage ended, working hard for another seven years when she got her PhD. She lives in Sienna for three years now, working in the university. She plays piano well and has a better voice than Clem. She sings in bars and has collected a following of fans.

Kate is coming on the twenty-ninth. The house is again a mess. It starts the day she leaves and is only cleaned again thoroughly just before she arrives. She is the only one this is done for, she is the only one who stays there. Clem notices that hours spent cleaning are necessary and this one big clean wouldn't take as long if the house was generally clean, but the hours spent cleaning generally far exceed the concentrated hours before his sister's arrival.

He felt the anguish approaching through his body. He was swearing constantly at many things, 'the need to do this.' He was struck by how crazy humans actually are. He was having a reasoned argument with himself, within himself. He found a third party, of himself, necessary to arbitrate and then it seemed like there was a forth part of him, looking in, having nothing to do with the argument.

He cleaned and scrubbed and washed. There would only be two or three more times to do this before he was free. Kate was crass, aggressive, annoying, right a lot of the time. As Clem arguments tended to involve the bigger picture a bit more often, the argument would flop, as it was hard to continue it into this realm with his sister.

Clem cleaned on. This time, his life was getting better. Funds increasing, slowly but increasing, he'd 'a work' in the bag. And was set about another. He'd trained himself for the year, just one year. It was dawning on him that the year for earning money was becoming so much about writing, reading, discovering, jumping to new facets of life, intriguing and as boring as they came.

The far reaching and meaninglessness of it all was what he was contemplating on the stairs as he brushed down assembled weeks of dust and debris. According to a planet, so very far away, who is Elvis? Who is Einstein? What is man? What effect will we ever have on anything? We have made it to the moon, depending on your belief that it actually happened.

'Like fleas off a drowning dog is it possible one day that we may skip on to a man-made craft, with the ability to survive, reproduce without any reliance on the Earth.

A couple of generations away, the need is not desperate yet. It is possible that in a thousand years, people will be born and die who have never been to Earth? If we make it that long. But to a star, the moon we are only a thing. Yes, it has the elements necessary for life… hmmm…' he thought. *'So as bacteria forms, from whatever equations are binding and thereafter life…'* He pauses again. *'What is the definition of life? When does something inanimate become living?'* He paused on the stairs and turned around, no one was there.

He googled the question and the first thing he came upon, after a few harry potter websites, was *Critique of "The Objectivist Ethics"*, was he going to 'have to read more?' he thought as he looked briefly at the thirteen parentheses lined out in front of him. *'As I'm sober.' 'Ow,'* he thought, *'people have been here!'* He found himself rambling through a lot of ethical questions and objections to the theory proposed.

He liked that Rand had pissed off so many people, how academics had disowned her. They're all playing a game too, vying for credentials, grants, kudos. What do they know of true thought? Do they get fed up along the way and start affairs or lose faith, do all philosophers lose faith? Walking the same halls day after day. Yeah, they might do a bit of reading and writing and thinking and logical hard thinking but if he's going through a divorce or separation how much of his mind is on the job in hand?

Clem jumped on to Libertarianism. Clem was a liberal, in name anyway. He was anti-state, anti-war, unfortunately the species hadn't got rid of all these follies yet. Globalisation, that demon word, was getting rid of a lot of what the libertarianists seemed to be prophesying. The recent mantra of Wall Street, Stock Market, CFD's, money has always been a carrot and will be for the foreseeable future. Companies pulling out of one country in favour of another, for smaller corporate taxes, cheaper labour costs, government grants.

In companies, there are ethics. There is a range, as in life, very ethical people, average and not very ethical. The thing is, to an individual, ethics standards vary. Some are conscious they are being ethical, others know they are not. Clem has seen himself hold both ends. It is easy to be ethical given circumstances where the price is cheap, the higher the price the harder it gets.

There are CEO's and high up members of companies and politicians all over the world who already have more than they or their children can spend. What keeps them involved? Nothing better to do? Don't know how to do anything else? Let's make more? 'I've something to contribute for the good'? different levels of 'good' depend on different levels of what that 'good' is. It is easy to be critical in hindsight, but Clem realises that he too has let others down and as much in decisions he has made or delayed to make. The big decisions by politicians and CEO's can have devastating consequences.

It's Tuesday, Clem goes up to mother. She's not well at all now and the repetition of the same questions is non-stop. She is barking, fighting for life. It has completely overtaken her. Gone now are the Tuesday-night prayers.

"Oh, Angel of God
My guardian dear
To whom God's love
Commits me here
Ever this night
Be at my side
Through light and dark

To rule and guide,

Amen."

His mother, when better able, would add her own personal requests at the end, "and bring Clemence up to me on Saturday for a spin," it annoyed him at first, another request for herself, at his expense. After a bit of thought, he could see that though her prayer was for her, it was also a benefit because if it came through then Clem would be alive and well next Saturday. Clem had told her along the way that he didn't believe in God, he hadn't yet figured out what to believe in yet. He was fine with still praying, he just put them down as 'wishes' now.

It would bug him for a second, when entering the nursing home, his mother would declare, "I've been waiting for you all day, Oh God sent you!" It was starting to feel to Clem that he had just driven up. What if he'd stayed at home, where was God then? There was something pushing him to go. To make it before four on a Saturday, was that God? If Clem had his way he'd have been long gone out of the country.

It was during and after one of their Saturday excursions, Clem realised 'he couldn't do this anymore, not this life' that was the tipping point. Three and a half years on, another Saturday, another tea and doughnut, another two hundred questions in the hour and a half to two hours. He had to divorce her. Her, and as much to do with her as possible, he just couldn't bare it any longer. This along with other factors boiled up enough fuel for him to use in order to cross that bridge, once and for all.

Was it the love for his mother that kept him coming up Saturday after Tuesday after Saturday, surprise visits or bringing her to appointments? Was that love for his mother? Amongst all the questions there were times she was great to be around. Fun, smart, loving and a rare time, wicked. Was it his love for her that kept him coming? Was it politics? Living in the family home, stipulated in his fathers will, was it the God inside him? When he lived outside the house for a year and a half he had still made those visits. Was there guilt involved? Would there be a huge guilt, to live with, if he let her down? Was it God all along that had been pushing him here? What was God up to? Was he like this with everyone or just Clem?

Clem had a coffee, cigarette and got back to more research. He already had made his mind up there wasn't a God, a God of the biblical sense, none that belonged to a religion but something still remained inside him, he really needed to search deeper. This was more interesting. Clem had become an evolutionist or 'fluffy atheist' as he liked to call it, this article went through the origins of life.

He waited for the end of it to say something like 'God is the answer' but it didn't. It went through the twenty amino acids needed to create bases proteins in order for life to commence. It drifted through nineteenth-century science and showed how twentieth-century science proved it wrong. The article ended with, 'we need another explanation for the origin of life.' This of course leads the way open for God but it gives science a fair chance too. Clem was just after leaving the 'God' side, he wasn't going to jump off the science wagon just yet.

Clem had his own ideas about heaven. Heaven was in a few places. Heaven, in many ways was the past. Everything is gone there. Like the coral reef. It is 'living' but made up of dead things. Made up of what has preceded everything, by people, by animals by every action that has ever occurred. That life is like a relay race. When then baton is passed, death arrives and that individual is no more but the baton keeps moving.

That person, when they were alive, has set in place equations that keep going, it was part of an equation that brought that 'thing', living or dead for whatever period of time, and its influence is carried forward. Heaven for certain, for Clem, is the now, the true most beautiful heaven of all. To taste it, feel it, live it. For after this, he believes there is no more for an individual.

No seeing loved ones again, no Gabriel's horn. This is it, and to have fear occupy it, perpetrated by whatever equation or force, is the robbing of everything. There is no need for pain in this world. That is where we must head as a species, the eradication of pain. As the species evolves and understands itself better and better the value of pain as an emotional feature must be diluted. *'Is it impossible not to miss or long for someone?'* he thought. Probably, if one day it is understood, maybe our senses aren't up to it yet! *'There will always be some element of pain,'* he finally accepts.

So why was he brushing the stairs? 'Dust to dust, ashes to ashes, funk to funky.' Clem smiled wryly to himself. That was the thing. Cleaning wasn't actually that terrible. There was something trance-like to it. Stroking, like rowing a boat. He'd drift off to a stream of non-threatening if a little disturbing thoughts.

Why was he here and why for the twentieth time was there a tiny little fragment of dirt in a little corner he couldn't get to. Though he knew he could get it and might, he'd find something smaller and he'd have to keep going on again. The best solution after many years and enough sense about this dilemma, was to see if it was clean from a certain distance.

Give something a significant number of sincere attempts, a few more than he would have been fine with, and to leave it at that. Beyond that point the reward was far smaller than the effort. That was cleaning. You could get something clean but it was never going to be entirely clean. The more you'd convince yourself you could, the more clinically insane one would become. That was the area for people with OCD, Clem had enough already without adding that to his resume.

He didn't like getting down on his knees in the kitchen either. The dirt was worse and he knew he was equally as bad at this as his father was at cooking. It wasn't his thing. Sweeping was okay, and washing ware was fine until dishwashers came along. He'd love the suds and warm water on his hands.

For shining furniture he blamed the particular object for not being able to look after itself. He hated how sometimes people would describe dirt, dust! Tell you everything about what it was, what was in it. That would send Clem imagining it in his head. It was never a nice thought, the sooner they'd stop describing it, the sooner something else would be able to filter into his mind. something prettier or weird, or just a little space.

He'd turn away and come back to that particular argument, only ever saying in his mind, that 'the dust was going to multiply, gang-up and kill him!!' He'd laugh a little to himself. 'Fucked up' realising as much about himself.

Bathrooms were okay. There was a lot of water there in the first place. The bulk of it was ceramic, tile or lino. A lot could be glossed over quickly, there was toilet paper as a ready-made disposable cloth and strong, powerful detergent would wreak a lot of havoc on them germs.

Clem didn't like spiders, he'd talk to them though, a little, once they were 'over there.'

A biggish daddy long legs had made the bath tub his home for a few weeks. Clem said 'Hi' to him now and again. At the start he didn't want him getting 'too big for his boots,' but a compromise was reached. The day however arrived that Clem had to clean the tub. He shrugged his shoulders at the spider and said, "that's life, what can I do?" He seemed a little too big to handle.

He turned on the shower head, it didn't dispense the water with great pressure and only dribbled toward the 'suck hole'. Clem raised his eyebrows at the spider. This time he reached for the main tap, just before turning it on he offered the spider a sincere, apologetic shrug, the palm of one hand opening in sympathy.

The tap opened and the water came flowing out with good pressure, it kept gaining ground toward the spider, soon it was turning his brown hair black. The spider reacted but the water kept chasing him. Clem felt something. A regret, embarrassment, guilt, remorse, and with a quick dive grabbed a tissue and trawled the spider out.

He was the spider's God for that second. For that week. Unless the spider had gone away to where Clem couldn't see him. Or something else might have got him. Clem realised he might have been too late but the spider had a chance now. The consequences of it Clem thought about briefly. That the spider, if he lived, was going to have feed on something. Not good news for them! Good news for whatever fed on these spiders.

For such a little act of 'whatever' was going to have consequences but in the grander scheme of things going to have such little relevance on anything. A lot like cleaning the house or driving a taxi.

Chapter 15

He extends this theory. The cost of repairing something because it is not kept clean or repaired the moment the opportunity arrives is more expensive generally. Sometimes, if the problem is systemic to an individual's asset then the cost can be truly great.

Clem drives a taxi. He has full faith that the car will not pass its reliability test in May. The cost of repairs or buying a new one does not justify the expense because it goes to something that will not yield beyond August.

Agga, a cool girl from a hotel, says to Clem, "your petrol light is on." It had been on for about ten minutes at this stage.

Clem was breezy this night and, exaggerating a little, replied, "the tyres are bald, the brakes don't work, I've no fourth gear and you're worried about a petrol light!!" He pauses. "…It's like what's going on and what's really really going on!!"

Christmas was quiet. Kate being in Italy, Harry and his family were in and out before three. Mother was weak, very weak but determined to make it to his sister's. In all, she ate a prawn. All she did was ask for her 'five o' clock' tablet and when that was given early at four-fifteen, she asked repeatedly when she could go home. Everyone knew it would be her last Christmas, and it seemed obvious her last few weeks and days were in the offing.

Christmas was nearly over. It had been quiet, really quiet, which seemed worse than dreary or anything eventful, even if something had happened in a bad way.

No great symbolism. Just dinner, a very nice one, a board game, drinks and some television. Not a great deal discussed. Little about the future, little about the past, nothing about the present. There was a difference. Something else mattered but it didn't matter because everyone's deck was different. It seemed they were in the middle of a shuffle.

Kate made it to Cork. Clem up all day from cleaning was exhausted. He collected her at the train station and they drove to mother's. Mother was perky, for a while. She was in darkness with the sun setting so early, convinced she had been in the dark all day. Clem and Kate explained what had happened. She refused their explanation. She had a terrible, sometimes deliberate, habit of dropping people in it. She asked Nisha, the staff nurse, "Why had they let her in the dark all day?"

New Year's day arrived, early morning. Clem looks after his regulars. Resolutions haven't got much of a mention but usually Clem's ones are all broken by the time he picks up a McDonalds at five thirty in the morning. He regrets it immediately. Not the breaking of every year's resolution but the taste of McDonalds breakfast menu. It's four euros ten cent with a nice coffee but the food is just stink.

The secret's out. After dropping Helen and Erin home he picks up a guy heading for town.

"This is it!" he says. "We turn to shit after this." he continues.

He's twenty-four, the same as Mariella.

"Are you a catholic?" he questions Clem presuming he is another.

"No, I'm a 'fluffy atheist'," Clem answers smiling. It's like the dimoxinil scene from *the Simpsons*, but Clem knows more. He needs to get it written and out there before it's all blown apart. He knows it's all blowing apart but he needs to invest quickly in a doctrine to profit from his ideas. Seven billion people. Others must have these ideas.

He'd known for a while now what John Lennon was on about in 'Imagine.' Was that why he was shot? Just a theory.

Chatting with Perma-culturists they seemed taken aback by his progress, he might just be still ahead of the game but if he keeps spouting lines of "did we think we were divinely chosen when we were monkeys" he's not going to have much to unleash… neither does he want to dismiss the band The Pixes.

Should he invent an end or stay the course? It needs to be out there quickly. With the modern speed of information, the opportunity may soon be squandered. He wrote to Mariella half past midnight, "All the best for 2012. (Vegas!... lucky b***h)" *'There's no need to be an asshole!'* he thought to himself.

So where is he now? What's his conclusion? Why are we here?

'This is heaven. Figure out what you really want. Don't blame…' and he pauses.

"Do I really want to go to Spain?"

"Yes!" Clem knows it will have its difficulties. It will be hot, extremely hot at times. There will be documentation and bureaucracy to deal with that will involve more waiting. And Madrid some days will seem like a pile of red-brown bricks as opposed to the open space and green of Cork.

And Ana warned him. Ana, a stunning girl of about twenty, with a camera around her neck in an Irish bar when Clem went to Madrid to meet Mariella the previous December.

Mariella loved him but at the same time was afraid of her life of him. She shafted him and when he showed some backbone and carried on without her, she couldn't believe it. He'd given her ample time to respond to his messages. He sent her an 'Adios' message on the Saturday and carried on without her.

He was drunk and she couldn't believe he'd done this to her. When his update of 'nice tree' was responded to in seconds by her, 'life is too short for me to stop'. He knew she was a coward. A full facial coward. She wanted but was afraid of her life. She'd left him down, badly. She was capable of it all the time.

Mariella, had come to the city and located him. With a gang of her friends, they saw him sitting at the counter, inside a bar finishing the end of a pizza. 'Has he spotted me?' She turned away quickly. She'd seen enough to make a judgement. He was okay, she thought, 'tall, big, half bald, not bad looking. She would have him... later.'

She hung around, with her friends and went to a few *copa* bars. She'd string Javier, along to an Irish pub. She'd figured for certain Clem would end up in there, he'd have to.

True enough, after a longer wait than Mariella had expected, near on closing time, he came in, got a drink at the bar and slumped into a spot on a couch around an eight-seat table. He looked around. The table had been relatively empty but the two Italian girls who had been sitting there were yet to return from a toilet break. She didn't like the place he picked, not one bit. The girls had been trying it on with guys all night and now they were returning to a miserably charming man. When they returned one sat across from him, the other right next to him.

He had them eating out of his hands in less than a minute. Mariella didn't know whether it was him or the girls' desire for flesh. Mariella had seen Clem look around and offer her a strained look, that turned briefly into a stare. She looked blankly away at nothing. Holding no conversation with Javier. She was in a semi trance.

Mariella had scaled the bar and she'd seen Ana. What she wouldn't have done to have jaws like that, but she took comfort in her blonde hair, it still set her apart, if only for a while. Clem faded from the conversation with the two Italian girls. It was clear he didn't want to talk to anyone. He just stared at the beer and whiskey and just gave an occasional glance around the room.

The camera, more than Ana, had caught his attention though. He tried to ask her a couple of questions but with the distance between them was hard for her to hear. Mariella started brewing inside. Clem leaned over to speak to Ana, Mariella was dying.

Relief, he'd returned to the couch, back hard and supported, it was clear he'd experienced no success. The distraught feeling inside her when Ana got up and sat across from Clem could not be measured. He was nearly old enough to be her father. Not nearly good-looking enough for her.

Mariella, couldn't look. She couldn't stop looking. They were talking the way she wanted to talk to him. Talk to anyone that way. He could see her body movements draw towards him and the worst thing was he didn't know how or why. Mariella crawled into herself. The Italian girls were coming back for more and without any trouble he was able to hold court with all three without even having the slightest bit of interest. The girls were playing with their hair, knees pointing to him like daggers. They were laughing and giggling.

It was far too much for Mariella, she ushered Javier to grab their coats. She couldn't wait to be out of there.

Mary his sister had once said to him, "because she can," Clem knew the full implications of it. He'd seen Carmen. He also knew that Mariella didn't know what Clem was gaining, he wasn't fully aware of it himself either, it was better that way. Clem would play the fool. He'd play it brilliantly. The reward was Mariella, if he could play it long enough, the real reward was Madrid, Spain, the bar, maybe an art centre, freedom. Mariella could be taken out of the equation, he loved her all right. The idea of her was the real love. Characters as all his life would change.

Back to life. Why was he here? He's here because this is heaven. It's not, why him anymore. It is him and what's he going to do with it? What would he like to gain pleasure and rid him of a lot of the tedium that surrounds his life.

Clem would like to fly, like a bird or discover beautiful dimensions as yet unknown. He'd like a drink, a lot of drinks. A few drugs, now and again, to get high. He found himself getting high sober now but many things drew him back, grounded him.

Conversations of small talk were ended but that meant they didn't last long.

In the breath of a day, like a dying gust, it was quiet again.

"Ah, shut the fuck up!" Clem lambasted at the radio. As the newish operator trained in the completely new one. Phones were ringing in the background. Clem was back in a slow-moving queue, the streets were quiet and it was time to contemplate again.

"At least it was 'this year'!"

Cigarettes had gone up as had the price of petrol at the pump. People were going to struggle. He'd dropped an elderly group into town who had just plain annoyed him. They chatted amongst themselves about going to Ennis for some 'sniff'. It was nonsense, nonsense, nonsense. Never going to happen. At least the shit Clem talked had a chance of coming through. Clem said nothing. Dropped them off and took the money.

Another girl just completely annoyed him. It was her voice, her mannerism her pure desperation for attention. She was just not attractive in many ways. It was her misfortune. She was kind, maybe funny, not really, it was just never going to happen for her. Mariella's voice had a question mark over it. He remembers it not being the greatest. It could get naggy.

Clem felt laws of attraction are a bit like that. You like someone, then you doubt you like them, then you find you really, really like them. The third segment needs a bit of patience though. When the opposite applies of disliking someone the gap between the second and third segment was not so long.

The night was going to be quiet. He'd already been home for two coffees and two pisses. It was going to be a long night, a long year and Clem could already see the 'sameness' strewn out in front of him. Many, many hours to kill. Clem was wrong. The night picked up around eleven and he was on the go until three. He wondered a little and realised he was just tired. Tired of this. Driving taxis, Ireland, the public.

He noticed two girls smiling, the night before, a girl being kind to a homeless person. He knew her face, it was a pretty one with long black hair. He'd talked to her a few times in the taxi, they'd built a rapport. He'd be glad the next time to have her in the taxi to remind her of her good deed. Which also reminded him to have a word with the little minx he knew, who danced in front of his car the night again previous.

A young lad got Clem to take him home. He was delighted with his local bar's refurbishment and new owners. Clem was at odds as to how the young man could be so enthralled by such an undeserving event. Clem thought, mind skewing up inside, was he like this? When he was younger? He knew he had been naive, still so, would a matter ever this trivial, have had him so enthused?

He acknowledges being wrapped up, until relevantly recently in such small binding matters. Things got to him.

He'd always wanted to escape this. Clem was wandering the streets of Zaragoza wondering when it would be his turn. He'd made a move to kiss a girl he asked directions from, she quickly rebuffed him. He made it to the nightclub, alone. He went downstairs and drank some Tim Bean. It was a boys' weekend away and his eyes were closed only an hour since he'd left home, thirty six hours earlier.

The Tim Bean got the better of him and he lost the race to the exit before the vomit from his mouth fell to the floor. He moved quickly outside, got sick some more, recovered himself and just opened his arms to look at the moon. He was praying to God or whatever, "when is it my turn?" He had sort of a drunk epiphany. Turned around and there she was. She was smiling, looking at him. He checked behind him to make sure. It seemed to be him.

She was smiling, beaming. He'd later think, did she catch him looking at the sky? He doesn't remember how the conversation started up. But he had 'a team meeting' in his head the seconds before they drew close to each other.

He told her he was a writer. "Better than Paulo Coelho." She was beautiful. Dainty. Full long blonde hair that went on forever. Clear beautiful tanned skin. He told Mariella and her friends he'd write them a poem. The girls managed to get a pencil or eyeliner and a piece of paper. Clem took them and waited for the words… they wouldn't come.

"I'm too drunk," he declared. "Or too tired!" "I'm exhausted… hold on, hold on! Nah! Nothing." The conversation went on but the girls had to go in.

Clem thought Mariella was magnificent and what a nice bunch of girls. Was about to leave it at that but another meeting took place in his head. *'Go in, you idiot. Go in and get something. A phone number. E-mail. Something.'* Clem turned around and paid another ten euros at the door. They hadn't seen him vomit on the way out and generally the Spanish bouncers' attitude is money is money.

Clem slipped up to the bar and passed Mariella on the way back with her gang in tow, her blue stringed top on show as her unzipped tracksuit parted by her sides. She seemed to give a wave of distain at a reference from a friend, “what about such a guy?” She passed Clem and they agreed to meet up in a part of the bar that they never knew existed. Her nose was kind of funny, nothing wrong with it but kind of funny.

Clem got a coke, the free drink which came with the entrance fee. He didn’t want to be spewing up in her company. He made his way slowly to where Mariella’s group wes. He was trying to pretend he wasn’t desperate but then again he’d really nowhere else to be.

He joined the group and they chatted, small talk, which Clem unusually didn’t prolong. He offered Mariella a drink. He came back with nothing. “Bar’s closed.” He offered her some of his, she sniffed it, “what is it?” she asked.

“Coke.”

“Coke and what?”

“Just coke.”

She thought, *‘he turned free alcohol down’*. He thought he’d shrug his shoulders instead of explaining he got sick.

The language barrier was tough. He offered her a cigarette. His box was empty bar one crooked white papered lonely.

“We’ll go halves,” Clem suggested. He passed her the lighting cigarette which she looked at with complete indignation. She let it fall from her hands deeming it not worthy to adorn it with the tiniest mull of effort.

They cajoled further on, poorly. The conversation wasn’t as ripe as earlier. The music just a little too loud. Clem asked her to chat a while, but a silence entered between the two. It seemed like Mariella plunged down a hole. At six foot he suddenly dwarfed her. He also got a clear view of her jaws for the first time. They were not attractive at all, indeed nearly hideous.

Mariella snapped, "Why aren't you talking to me!!" Clem had to think quick, inside he was laughing at her temper, he really liked it.

"Because I'm going to talk to you forever!" He knew as soon as he said it that he'd jinxed himself. It was better than what the devil inside his head was telling him to say. He promised himself there and then never to mention the 'J' word, how that was going to be tested in the following years.

Clem decided he better look at her ass. Mariella's friends were watching so in order that they could say something to her after he started to take a peek. He made it quite obvious. It was actually a fine, fine piece of design. Clem was wasted. Mariella was fairly tired too, both with most of their senses, they were okay together… just there.

The club ended. Clem had got her e-mail, after pushing for her phone number. He'd be on the plane that day to Ireland, Mariella on the coach back to Madrid. As she walked away he shook her hand. The Spanish way of kissing on the cheek passed over as Clem was a titler for formality with a person he liked. As Mariella and her friends walked away Clem said 'goodbye' and 'bye' in a variety of different tones and pitches, like a crowd of friendly people individually saying goodbye.

She was gone. Clem had been in Barcelona the previous night and met Brunai early in the morning. A pretty, English girl of Pakistani extraction, they had a chat and Clem got her e-mail. It was like so many other meetings. Whether they ended up in bed or not was never his main priority. Clem had done this before. Away or back home in Ireland. Indeed since he first started chasing girls at fifteen years of age.

There were discos in Cork for summer students coming from Spain, Italy and France.

Clem went swimming one day in June and as he remerged from the water to wipe his eyes, two visions of feminine godliness draped their bodies against the pool wall. From head to toe, they were heaven. Long jet-black hair, sallow skin, perfectly shaped teenage bodies in black swimsuits leaving him in a state of awe. "I've got to get one of them," he burbled through the water in his mouth.

Clem met a girl Sandra, from the Basque Country in one of the discos. He met her again the following summer in the same place. They kissed the second summer, no more. A list started to form from there. By now, forty, he had had many impossible long-distance relationships, as many times hypothetical as real.

He knew himself, from a long time ago, why. He wanted out of it. Here, Ireland, his family, his home.

He had desired so many different women at different times. As a percentage he did well. He'd a few things going for him. He was a tall, slim, broad shouldered reasonably handsome man. He was kind but a tad quirky which ruined his chances with a few but had others remarkably intrigued. His voice was fine, lyrical and he'd a devil of a wit at the end of his tongue. He was an avoider though. He just didn't want it when it was offered. It was never right. There were a few who he could have worked it.

There were two who stood out though. Valentina and Mariella. One sixteen years after the other. No doubt to Clem, which one was the right one for him.

Chapter 16

And in This Room, This Is the Look at the Walls Room

Ana had warned him, that so many of these people were fakes! It took Clem a while, but thirteen months later, he came upon the theory that perhaps 'we all are fakes'. With the mind ever increasing in its ability to understand and compute, were we starting to leave our bodies, as remarkable an instrument as they are, behind? We turned our ingenuity to create machines to compensate for the lack of sheer power or subtlety in our bodies.

Wouldn't we like the ability to fly? Without aid, free. Why haven't we grown wings? Have our minds set that in process, or are our minds just worried about themselves as a separate entity within ourselves? 'How cruel would that be? If we figured out our minds were just using us, using our bodies, manipulating us… *'Clem, that's nonsense,'* Clem agreed.

So why hasn't our mind got around to this? Is it impossible? Is the best thing the calculation of the creation of a machine to fill the desire that our bodies cannot fulfil? Is the structure of our body enough? That's it, no better. No second liver, third kidney. Why no 'three of anything? 'Twos and ones, twos and ones… five digits but twos and ones of everything else. No threes! None that Clem could think of. 'Teeth, bones,' 'not like that'. Has the mind made its mind up, 'there's no more to do here!' has evolution just stopped? Did we really come from monkeys? How long is time? How long is a million years?

Clem grabs a calculator. 'A million years is twenty-five thousand of what I've lived already.' Over fourteen and a half thousand days. He was a baby, child, teenager, young adult and now middle age. He's evolving before his very eyes. What is that? What force has it, what built in equation has it, that we die? Our minds don't want it, it's the end of that too. It's in all of nature. Better and brighter is coming up behind, it's not unfair. But if we are so in control of ourselves then why don't we reach an age of forty, fifty, whatever and something takes us off, away to another planet? What genetic feature has it that we die?

Is that what the brain is working on, evolving to? How to get to survive to one hundred, two hundred, a thousand years? Is it preparing a better seed within us for reproduction? Why then does it offer me the choice to smoke? Drink? Take drugs? Drive badly? Jump through something that one doesn't know what's on the other side? What's intuition? Is that a gamble? Is it a subconscious ability to calculate the risk percentage of a certain activity and send it forward to our conscious brain? Why have we the ability to be so stupid? Just stupid, not illogical or irrational or abstract… just stupid.

Why can we sense ourselves doing something we don't want to do? Being somewhere we don't want to be? Sometimes from external forces, sometimes from curiosity. Why are we superstitious? Humans are weird, Clem feels he's weird.

Stimulation now was less served by food, sex, conversation. Already the attraction of two minds on a provoking plateau was the height of stimulation for Clem. He was getting high, 'dark high' on all this thinking.

A storm raged outside. Clem took the night off. His body had been demanding of him for a while now. The winds ravaged around the house. He was glad he didn't live in a cave. Still no move from Mariella. He'd been discussing with Kate about planetary waves and gravitational waves. Kate gave satisfactory answers, she has a PhD in the thing. It amazed Clem what was at work in this world. Recently, he calculated the Earth travels at one thousand miles an hour on its axis. Over ten million miles a day through space and within the Earth's general domain, there are so many equations taking place. The physics of the planet are truly remarkable.

The more he researched the more it intrigued him. He'd be glad to leave it alone and return to the guitar. He'd be glad to be able to get drunk and socialise again.

As he smoked a cigarette in the garage, house rules with Kate around, he said to himself, "there's no way you're getting over twenty grand." He was hoping it would be cash. The stocks, which rallied a little that day, were not included. He knew mum was dying and the house would be split. That would add to his lump sum. He figured he'd have a decent sum leaving for Spain or with back up in certain quarters.

Then returning to the plight of people under a particular weather pattern as they look up to something into the sky or something from within them or within someone else to save them, their property, their crop, their life, waiting for God to interject. It was a weather pattern, a simple weather pattern. Harsh, severe, extreme. Yet, in all, a weather pattern.

'What in God's name set off this fire? Forest fire, house fire, etc., a series of conditions involving oxygen, heat and carbon.

Why has God let me lose my job? Because of poor business decisions, 'then he is the devil'. Because that product does not need to be produced anymore.

It went on, Clem was glad his cigarette was finishing, he could return to the house and exit the path on which his thought process had trickled, he knew it would be back. It was forging a solid road in his mind.

He dabbled the lit end of the cigarette under the drip from the leaking roof, looked at it and threw it toward the bucket. It drew him the launch, slightly crooked, the flight as it meandered in the air, there was nothing he could do about it now, it was down to the gods, well, it used to be. It was physics now but the lure was still there, as it funnelled its way to the bucket.

Would it miss and fall to the ground, the price being he'd have to pick it up or would it go straight in? It cavorted with the lid of the bucket, trying to dive in but alas, it had reached the point where the ground was its destination. Clem looked at it, mouth a tad disdainful, turned around and went back inside, *'I'll get it later, not like it's going to detonate and cause a nuclear holocaust'.*

Inside away from Kate, many things were immensely more pleasurable than being in Kate's company, not that her company was always that bad, but for the times she was there, many things more pleasurable or less uncomfortable. Clem went to work.

As he drove around, he started to expand on the idea of "there's nothing I can do about it now." It confused him how so many people his own age, even younger were resigned to things. It felt really odd, Clem was really only at the starting line and here were people beaten, finished not even looking for something. The cliché Mariella had written about 'life being too short,' stuck in his mind.

“Life is long!” he spoke profoundly. “Too long to be doing the same shit.”

For the people who thought it was as good as over, he avoided his own story. Unless they moaned way too much, then he’d stick, *‘stupid fucking moaners,’* that blind moaning really annoyed him, that ‘over the top self-pity moaning’ he’d a guy once, out for a work night, bargaining the fare for a long job at a really short price.

Clem agreed, that ‘thing’ inside him again. The man had a basic job, been made redundant, his girlfriend was expecting and the mortgage for the house, heading to half the value he had paid for it, was three months overdue. Clem had sympathy for him and let him do some wimping. The customer went through the list again, this time adding the cable T.V. bill being five months overdue. That got Clem, that really got up his nose.

“You and your generation, with your…” and Clem ranted, “ye need a kick up the hole!!” Who was that side of Clem? It surprised him, a grown up inside of him? Clem could well be on his way to the bookies tomorrow. He was mostly losing his own money. Was Clem just finally learning?

As Clem drove round, things would enter his mind. Mostly it was only a few things, many times, he much preferred little entering his head. He liked moods. Dark moods, happy moods, somber moods. Depending on the music or the customers or the weather. He liked that about night driving, more solace, different. Sometimes when he was in a mood a customer would disturb it. But so often he found them joining in the mood. For a bit of the journey the mood would prevail and then it would rush to Clem’s head ‘that he was only pretending,’ particularly if it was on the darkish side and would proceed to do 'stand up' for the rest of the fare, then they were gone and he could return to the mood, slightly darkish, 'melancholic' Mariella once wrote.

Clem checked up Melancholy, but he preferred 'Sanguine.' He settled for somewhere between the two.

Why had so many people 'resignation' written all over their face? Granted it was nights he drove and one's going to get more of it. It was really just a phase though. Less and less of them got into the taxi over the past six months. The truth was probably simpler, people who were resigned had run out of money and couldn't afford a night out. The hard startling cold truth fact.

Was it good for Clem to tell someone whose house and car were being repossessed, "oh! By the way… there is no God." Naturally the way phrases stick to the mind, the temptation to follow up that statement with, "but Allah." But as relevant to a person in such a position might be the words 'tough shit' might have been as sincere.

His relationship with his mother was very loving. They gave and gave and gave to each other. Clem had entered divorce proceedings with her at the latter part of last summer. He had to go. She understood. They had a few poignant moments, one of them as he took her for her 'Saturday spin' along the lower harbour road.

"Will you give me my tablet?"

"I will love."

"What time?"

"Five o' clock,"

"Okay."

"Are we going for a cup of tea, Clemence?" mother asks.

"Yeah."

"Where?"

"Just down the road a bit," Clem answers.

"Okay."

Silence for a few seconds.

"Will you give me my five o' clock tablet?" It's four o' clock.

"I will, mam," Clem answers.

"Will we get tea and a doughnut?" mother asks.

"Yeah, just down the road," Clem adds trying to save another question.

"Will I be back for my tea?"

"You will, mam, your hair is lovely."

"Is it?"

"Yeah, really nice, when did you get that done?"

"Wednesday, fifteen euro."

"Really nice."

"Will you give me my five o' clock tablet, Clemence?'

"Ah mam!! Will ya stop." Clem asks.

"Okay, I'll say no more."

"It's a lovely day." Clem claims.

"Will you give me my five o' clock tablet?"

"Emm!" Clem answers drifting off in his mind, looking out at the setting autumn scene. The road transfixes him as they drive by.

"Will you give me the five o' clock tablet?'

Clem hears her. "I will, mam!!"

"Will I be back in the bungalow for my tea?"

Clem raises his eyebrows, half-perplexed, half-wryly, shrugging in his mind.

"Yeah, mam," he says placating.

It's four minutes past four. Clem is vacant. It's not so bad now. The day is coming when this will be done. He realised after many many Saturdays that he couldn't live with the braying, the constant braying of insane, mundane questions. It represented more. A lot more. 'Are you busy tonight?' 'What's it like for you now?' 'What time are you finished?' 'What time did you start?' 'You only get out of something what you put in to it.' 'It's a job.' 'Why are you going to Madrid, sure there's no Irish there,'

"Will you give me my five o' clock tablet?"

"I will, mum."

"Will you ring me every Tuesday and Saturday when you get to Spain, Clemence?"

"I will, mum."

"I'll have my phone charged up for you."

"Thanks, mum."

"Will you miss me, Clem?"

"I will, mum."

"You have to go, don't you?" She stretches out and grabs his hand on the gear stick.

"I have to, mum... I have to." He offers her a look, he's decided.

"I'll miss you, Clem."

"I'll miss you too, mum."

A little silence.

"Can I have my five o' clock tablet?'

"Yeah, mum."

"Will we be back to the bungalow for my tea?"

"Ahhh mam!! …yeah!" Clem answered with a sigh.

Clem thought about charity workers. Hospital staff, ambulance crew, police. Things people never see or take for granted that they deal with on a constant basis. He thought of the individuals behind the uniforms, in the skin. He considers himself giving, kind. Not as he once was but feels he's on that side.

He tries to contemplate the mindset of people who constantly give, like Mother Teresa and her nuns, just giving constantly. To be of that mind. Then others, who might have on their mind 'oh! Look at me, I'm caring?', he'd ask that question of staff a few times and found a fair portion of it to be true, as of an opinion. He also considered people who thought it would be 'a good job' but were completely sick of it now. Or those who thought of it as 'just a job' and got the hell out of it. He'd respect for all of them, because the care was provided. To the person who needs the help that was the most fundamental thing of all.

When in need, real need, one doesn't care how old you are, gender, colour of skin, your politics, philosophy, attractiveness, kindness. They need to be cared for right there and then, with that Clem had respect.

Clem went home to watch the television, briefly going to bed for two hours but he got up after thirty minutes. Shouldn't he be out working? That had gone. That running out the door. Pushing himself through before he got a chance to think, *'hold on, just half an hour,'* he'd worn himself out.

He decided to consciously give it one big push from the end of January. Twelve hours a day married to the car. It was closing, next year would soon be 'this year,' January would be quiet, the whole year from an economic standpoint looked dreary. Two thousand ten and eleven seemed to be a false dawn, 'the worst is over', 'green shoots of growth are appearing on the horizon,' were far off echoes now. 2012 was shaping up to be of holocaustic proportions.

The council's workers were pissed off, down money. The cops were pissed off, down money. Nurses, teachers, general operatives. Bills were still bills but getting bigger and pay packets smaller but yet still no mobilisation. No movement from the masses. People were giving up, blaming everyone while taking it up the ass. Why were they here? Gone, the holidays, changing the car every two years, the fancy dinners out, the extension to the kitchen, the forty-inch plasma, the pay per view channels.

Some took up walking, evening classes, many, if they could, ran away. Clem could see it, the crap his mother and father went through in the eighties was back, worse, a bigger ghost. He imagined the houses tonight, people behind the doors, one thing on their mind. Mortgage, electricity bill, gas bill, school uniform, clothes for the kids, food. It had been with him growing up, the tension all over the house, the day someone comes home and says, "I've lost my job." A terror, seeming to be the worst thing in the world. Worse than cancer or a tumour.

The nights of men around his own age getting into the taxi, saying, "the wife left me, with the kids," just grew and grew. Who would they go to now? "What use am I?" for others it was liberating, a relief, a freedom, a chance to go with someone else. Women bored with their husbands, sat in front of the television having to go upstairs and sleep with 'the pig' later. Biding their time, waiting for a bit of freedom from the overbearing presence of him. Any excuse to get out, stay out, it was rife. Some women were worse than any man.

Some of the customers would ask Clem:

"Married?"

"Nah."

"Kids?

"Nah."

"What are you going to do?"

"I'm heading off to Spain."

From there, the conversation would meander. From in a roundabout way "you loser" to "how did you know?"

"Because we're all gonna DIEEEEEEE!!" he'd sometimes end depending on how the conversation went.

Clem knew he'd been lucky not to end up in a home like he was encountering more and more of. It was like he'd been through it, as much from what he'd grown up around but from what he'd lived with, inside himself. He wanted to make that jump too, "for better, for worse," for a while, "let's see if we can work this", "you and I". He owed himself that. He believed in true love but that just runs out of steam sometimes. He'd love to try it, longer, realer.

Clem had been talking to Chloe. She'd been listening to a radio show about God.

"They had one group of scientists who believed in God and another group who didn't," she started.

"That's what I'm actually thinking about right now!" He hated that. Other people talking about God. That was his thing. Let him finish first and he'll get back to you. He divulged parts of what he was learning.

"You know they haven't even proven that evolution is true yet!!" Clem knowingly contributed.

"Well, babies heads are getting bigger!" Chloe retorted. '*Shhssh*' Clem thought in his head. Chloe gestured toward her pelvis. '*Eeek!*' Clem thought.

"Babies heads are getting bigger, that's why they're having more trouble giving birth in the first world. In the developed world it's not so much of a problem." Clem didn't like the picture it was forming, '*remove image… ahh, a field of wheat.*'

"You know the equations that go into making one baby are so huge, is that a miracle? How come there is

Seven billion of us? Is it the one or the seven billion that is the miracle? What relevance do we have to something far, far away?" Clem asked.

"That's life! The baby needs the mother!!" Chloe answered.

"The baby doesn't need the mother," Clem interjected. It caught him as much as it did her. It was cold. He didn't like it at all. He could see the thought happen inside her.

"The baby needs the mother to…" it realised itself in her mind, as it did in Clem's. The words had left her like a bark.

"Something comes along and replaces her," Clem added, neither meaning to, or not. A horrible truth had revealed itself. "No one is needed!!" It saddened Clem for a while as he drove around later. 'A baby needs to be born,' not necessarily true. Indeed, not true at all! A baby is born, that is true, it needs to be cared for, for a little while, that is also true. Clem knew he was lying, covering up, he tripped on to the easier truth. It cannot feed itself or defend itself. That baby needs these assistances to survive. Whether it be from the birth mother or a surrogate. It can also die at any stage.' Clem needed to stay cold on this, matter of fact, logical, impersonable. He'd lost it, his train of thought had slipped. He'd felt a fundamental line had slipped again.

The answer to 'not one individual is needed… so we're all needed,' had broken down. He'd jumped too far ahead again. "This is dark, Clem!!" he suggested to himself in his mind. "I know," he responded.

So all the loves, possible girlfriends, it didn't matter which one, just once someone had 'the love' or the far flung grandiose notion of it. Well, 'the love' yes, but somewhere better than others, more natural, more chemical, more wonderous. With some it was a lot less than being a chore. A lot less, 'Clem has a girlfriend, so he's okay,' with some of them it was good to be around. Fun, painful, easy, hard. Is that the difference between being a biological mother as opposed to a surrogate? A few biological mothers are just awful. For some children it would be better to have a surrogate. So it becomes a 'quality issue!!' Quality of life? *'What's your quality of life like, Clem?' 'Big picture great, small picture boring,'* he replied in his mind.

'So that means, as we stand at present, not good.' "When you put it that way… yeah," he answered loudly. It wasn't that parts of him knew things weren't going to change in due course. He pictured himself, having a drink, sitting back somewhere in the quiet of a morning or the height of a festival night, sipping a beer, nodding away to himself in his own quiet world. Content to be where he was, happy just being there watching the bubbles float up the glass, drawing him away into a trance where absolutely no thought would resonate. He loved that feeling. Had that feeling, enjoyed that feeling, wanted it again. This was not the time but there was a definite date. He'd already made the conscious decision if the bar was not making money, he'd drink it under the table, into a stuper, to death. '*What a way to go!'* in that mind frame, not caring, relaxed. That was a worse case scenario, *'what a great worse case!!'*

Chapter 17

He wishes he could write as quick as he can think, or think as slow as he can write. He was jumping from one point to another and before he could spoon a thread that would allow him to develop it, the original thought was gone. It happened in his schooling days. He'd read back over something and there would be five words missing, six words missing, he jumped randomly between thoughts that would not find themselves coherently on the paper.

He got low grades in language, geography, history. It was a time constraint. His writing was poor in such constraints. Yet he managed to win two poetry prizes and was part of the debating team. Being frank, Clem would be honest enough to admit his knowledge of events was far behind those of classmates.

Clem looking after Christoffe, a private early morning customer, drives along the deserted streets, feels he missed nothing the previous night. On the news it is reported that a young man who died eight days after an assault donated his organs. Five people picked up the organs and their lives are improved or saved. A young three-year-old in England is resuscitated back to life by an air ambulance after being dead for six minutes. It touches Clem.

He doesn't like gore or thinking of it. A few times he's blanked out talking on the subject. *'What are we for?'* he ponders. Governments set up these social programmes to benefit humans. We are all moving in the same direction. Poverty may still be around but it is becoming more and more distant. In all this, there seems a greater communal good.

All this thinking, where was it leading him? What was he doing to himself? Like being back in the bedroom. The bedroom, sky blue woodchip wallpaper, the hanging side of the bunk bed stop, never screwed back into position, burnt from the fire those many years ago.

He imagined back there, he remembered, physically it was just upstairs, just above his head. He hadn't gone in there in years, yet he'd stayed there so long. Just looking at the blue painted woodchip wallpaper, doing that math equation that ran and ran, dreaming about a girl or two on his mind. Dreaming about somewhere, away. Never ending. It went on forever.

Writing those poems and those songs, that seem so corny now. Childish. He always grew up later, stayed living in the dream, the running equation. How did he fall back here? What ghost was left? What was to vanquish? Was that it? Did he have to return and free himself from some point in the past? Was he going back there, to himself? Was that why Clem sent that letter? To be opened in ten years time when he was seventeen, when he was big and strong?

Was that it? A personal rescue of his young self? He remembers the start of the letter. That drawer, that room. A refuge, a prison. Nothing amazing, just a room.

'Dear Clem,

I know you're big and strong now and probably married and happy but remember me, this time…'

Clem eyes welled, he stopped. He acknowledged, he didn't overcomplicate it, didn't over-sentimentalise or at least he stopped quickly. He remembered crumpling it up a few days later and destroying it but he knew what it was about.

Why was he there, then, as a child? What was his reason for being here, on Earth? For Clem to remember that letter? What did he see? No matter…

It seems that every generation is a generation born too soon, probably two generations too soon. Those that get a grip of life, realise what little time they have left to plough. Others constrained by love, guilt and fear. Fear is dissipating in modern society and it seems to Clem that the whole of humanity seems to be heading inextricably towards the 'Dark Forest.'

What we find there may be as underwhelming as the 'wizard' in the wizard of Oz. Soon, with no one to tell us what to do except ourselves, what wall will be around in his 'brick analogy' theory. Love is great but is so often used as a weapon. The fear of losing love being greater than losing life. There are so many loves, feelings, bonds, emotions that do not retain a true worth in life.

It might be off putting at first. Like the airport in his hometown. A spanking new terminal to replace the old one which lay below. In a way, the old terminal took on a character of its own. It started to, not glow, but hold something stoic. Its ugliness was turned oddly beautiful next to the new building. Is that what would happen to religion, would it turn into a fable?

He was fed up of calling people 'dumb'. He'd tried hard to stop it. He wanted to stop generalising. He wasn't that way. Some other party had influenced him. He'd picked it up, he knew better.

Customers getting into the car and others. ‘People this’, ‘people that’, ‘they’, ‘everybody’. Was it just his car? Was it just this city? Was it the world over? He couldn’t have a conversation with everyone. He just found a lot of customers missing it. Missing themselves. ‘Politicians this’, ‘bankers that’. He asked customers many times, “what are you going to do about you?”. And off they would start blaming ‘people this’, ‘look what they done to the economy.’

“What the fuck is wrong with people,?” Sometimes during his thinking they’d come annoyingly to his mind. Then, there would be a hush and an individual would pop out and say, “you’re okay with,” and Clem would give them a quarter grin. They’d understand, it’s not you as individuals, he hadn’t got to the annoying one’s.

He wasn’t against people. He felt they just misrepresented so much. Clem was learning how much he was guilty of it too. He just wanted to think away, put things together and leave it at that. He’d be back soon.

Enough, he was starting to roll his eyes up to heaven, out of view. He’d got in enough trouble already with the company. With the dirt of his car and the depth of his tongue, he was already prohibited from picking up at two hotels. Some customers liked him though.

He’d built a decent relationship with the father of the girl who owned the company. He didn’t use it as a negotiating wedge but it bought him a little leeway. They talked on a variety of different subjects, both had expansive, inquisitive minds. He learned a little from him during their year and a half of Monday nights.

David, the base manager, was very direct. Earlier that year a uniform had been deemed mandatory. Like school children they were marched in for inspection. Clem was one of the last to comply. He'd only one company shirt, given to him free, a split all the way across the sole of his left black shoe. The water soaking his feet when it was wet. A navy jumper without any company logo on it. He'd picked up a few black pants for seven euro a pair.

When he was called in for an inspection, he'd open the boot of the car and pick out the bits and pieces he needed to put on before going in. As soon as he got a chance he'd switch them again. One morning, because it was necessary for hotel work, a concierge complained him for changing his shirt at the set down outside the hotel. It was five thirty in the morning, with no one around he found it necessary to complain. Clem found it necessary to object but ended up being out of pocket.

In order to generate finances for his move to Spain he decided to comply. He would wear the uniform all the time now but never wash it, until he himself couldn't stand the smell anymore.

He didn't know whether to be ashamed or proud of his car. It had seen only one hoover since July, or the body a wash. He was collecting many so called 'dignitaries' from the two best hotels in the area. Clem guessed that they knew after a few minutes, they were getting into 'one of them' cars.

For some of these guys and even more of the girls, though they were less in number, for their gain of wealth and status, they were married to a strict fairly narrow-minded regimen. Bullets propelled from a gun, no meandering until the very end, until they got lodged in something. Others, relying on intuition and a factor of skill and creativity were really nice to deal with. Wide varying conversations about everything that took place.

A 'lucky dollar' was given by a wealthy, well to do sort, who shared poetry of E.E. Cummings. Clem gave an experience. He was changing though, he was ceding physically. 'Was he selling out? Ultimately, yes!' But he was seeing things in a new light. He was figuring how to implement change in other ways. It was possible to change things. To teach people there are other things, other ways, that they're not stuck in holes. A hole is only a hole for as long as you want it to be. Clem had been in a hole most of his life, imagined or not. Finding a way, finding a solution, finding an escape.

He was nearly out now. Nearly away from everything that had held him. Just play the game a little, pay a little more lip service, a little longer, that prize was getting closer and closer. *'Do the quiet thing.' 'Stop mouthing off,' 'keep your mouth shut.' 'Patrickience... just a little more.'*

Clem was getting better at the above but it was so much in him. That fight, that spirit. It was nice putting the blues and browns away. First under the 'hooky watch set' to iron them out and then the empty golf club cover. It was adding up. If the need, even now, he could nearly make a go of it with what he'd saved. The bar would be smaller, but he'd still manage it, play guitar. Give some English lessons. It mightn't be the highs of Malasaña or Chueca but it would be warm and balmy suburbia. Stick at this though, for the duration, and it would be crazy nights in Malasaña and Chueca. A bit of madness, a bit of Carnivale, ModoVida.

He felt it, smelt it, sensed it. Mariella would walk in one day. Dependant on his mood, they made out straight away or he was telling her, 'get lost', 'too late,'. He liked to dream of that, not often because it was all about slipping those 'blues' and 'browns' under the watch set.

When he came back from his drift or wasn't rolling his eyes up at customers or getting involved in philosophical debates or dealing with mother, it was generally about why are we here? He'd give out to himself about having started it. He would tell himself to quit, *'leave it alone,' 'you don't really need this,'* was it really going to do that much for him, did he really need to know?

But he'd started and he'd stay the course until he got to the end but it was wearing on him, really wearing on him. Was it as obvious to others as it was to him or the other way round? He could hear himself, the echoes, he'd give a look to himself inside his mind. He was good company to himself. Not now. A bit deluded.

He was able to pull himself up generally if he went too far with his mouth or an action. His mouth was usually the culprit. He didn't like it, telling others how to live their lives. He had accidents,

"Go and see the world! Never mind Canada, Australia, United States! The world."

If only he followed a few of their examples himself. On airport runs he was dropping people who were going. Sometimes they were off to the same apartment near Malaga or the Algarve for the hundredth time.

"I'm off to Spain."

"Where?" a customer would ask. "But there's no Irish there?"

'Thank Christ! or at least not like you, there's not!! Narrow minded…' he thinks, before answering, "enjoy your trip!"

"Thanks!"

There were others though. Two in one morning.

"Where are you off to?"

"Stoke."

The customer didn't have a huge hangover because he'd only put down his last bottle of beer as he was getting into the taxi.

"Cool, what's happening there?" Clem asked.

"I'm a crystal glass sculptor!"

"My kinda guy!!"

The conversation was off, a common level… they understood each other immediately. He was a weirdo, he was brilliant. The customer before was off to the Rugby World Cup. 'Another one' Clem assumed. 'Look at me, I'm going to the world cup!'

"There's a girl from Argentina and we meet up in different places all over the world. We travel together for a while until we have to head back home. We have to save every penny until we get together again!!" he revealed.

"Absolutely crazy but I love it!! Will ye live happily ever after?" Clem enthused.

"I don't know, man, we'd like to but she can't get a visa to come here and there is no work in a lot of places for me!!"

"You keep trying, man, you keep trying!!" Clem loved that, loved it.

Of course he put his foot in it on occasion, like when touring Americans were heading to the airport and he was listing out the fabulous places they should visit like..

"South America, Paris, Brussels, Afghanistan…" he wasn't having a go at them or U.S. foreign policy, it just slipped out.

These customers were a good lift to another ordinary night. People doing their thing, 'on a journey,' *'hate that euphemism'* Clem quickly quipped. He didn't like Coelho, he was a little jealous of him, sure. Not in awe of him but a good deal jealous. He could see how people could get 'the journey' thing, he felt it a little himself but he truly felt it fell a little short. *'Isn't that what you're on?'* he quipped against himself, *'oh! shut up.'* Maybe it was because Clem hadn't done it or hadn't found it or it wasn't honestly him. It felt a tiny bit religious, he didn't want to be stealing from Hitchens either but he was growing more and more to like him.

Chapter 18

Clem was irate. Mariella had him, again. His blood was boiling as she wound him up with a status update. She'd received a gift from her friends in Madrid and plastered the thanks and 'I love you' all over. She left a jibe with, 'buaa… you just can't write it." A definite attack on Clem with lots of Ls with purpina, relating to another guy, on it. She was a thundering bitch.

He'd seen her attack other guys with bazooka size bombs. Clem laughed when it happened to them but he'd been hit more often than anyone, yet still came back for more. What irritated him was that his book of poems was to be published within ten days. He was going to send a copy to Mariella, and would still do it but really now he'd had enough of her bitterness, he knew in truth things were not quite wrapped up yet.

He wasn't going to sign. He wasn't going to give her that ammunition. She'd seen the messages though. The nearly two hundred messages though. The wimpy ones. The panicky ones. The begging ones. How'd he ever face that? What was he up to? He didn't have the hand to play hard ball. He didn't have the cards to call her bluff.

He didn't want it. But she got to him, he responded in kind. She'd react, submit, concede and then slay. Was that how he was to play it? Despite himself, hard, cold. It wasn't in him, yet. It's fake, it's a game. Just another part of the big sell, couldn't she climb higher than that? Couldn't she wait till his stock was higher? Then Clem was Clem, if his stock got higher, he'd walk away. *'Maybe a relationship of convenience is better,'* could either accept such?

She was a bitch anyway, just now, for the longest time. Is that what they turn into? Was Kate just a bitch? Were so many of them lost, lost in relationships and lives they detested? Was this their fight, their gripe, their bark? Was everything different now? The modern world! Full of so many new things, empty of others. Was this honesty? Was it waking up and seeing things as they are now? Was loyalty dying? Loyalty to something else, was 'the self' greater now?

He'd wrote to her once about 'trusting her,' she wasn't having any of it and threw it back in his face. 'What a crock!' not from her, him. What were they buying at all? Weren't all the movies and television shows he'd seen telling him to do this? 'What a crock?' he needed out of that so bad. He still wanted something romantic, was romance dead? What was the new romance? A giant orgy of 'self', free from suppression, free from 'fitting in'? what good would that do the species? Was it time to forget the species and just run? Run from responsibility of reproduction. *'They're my genes and I'm keeping them!!'*

'Let's just stop. Stop the inevitable. Never mind who looks after us before we die, just run with this, all together as one. Complete world contraception!! Let's copulate until it all falls off!' "That gets tedious too!" he interrupted. As the economy impacts, and impacting it is and people have less and less to dispose on materials, it draws upon them. The question. Time on their hands. Old people around the estate. 'I WANT!!' 'What does anybody really want?'

For some, they are lucky, what about Clem? What does he really want? 'A monkey off his back!' 'The NEXT?' whatever 'the NEXT' is? Is that life? A series of growing NEXTS and then decreasing NEXTS. To find that ultimate summit, that ultimate 'NEXT'. Who finds the ultimate NEXT? Religionists, is it delusional? If that's the ultimate NEXT, they have to hang in there until the end. Is the poetry book the ultimate achievement for Clem?

What was the ultimate NEXT for a child who dies after an hour? To make it to an hour and one minute? What's the ultimate NEXT for someone who lives until a hundred and twenty years of age? To live until they're one hundred and twenty years and one minute? It doesn't seem so logical. So life after a certain point becomes redundant. Somewhere, something, must exist in a life that means something, means something more, more than God. Reproduction? Is it really? Is that it? Reproduce, die off. Fuck and die? A visit to a sperm bank. A ten-minute deposit. A life's meaning in that? Is there something greater, for 'the self', for 'the species'?

When does that 'NEXT' come along? Which is the true NEXT? The one that frees you, that frees Clem? That tells him why he's here, that tells him there is a God, there is no God. What is that 'thing' that deletes God. That one meaning, event, simple or huge epiphany. Are we meant to grow wings and fly? Is that it? Clem was confused. He needed a break from it. He was getting nowhere, *'this is useless,' 'no point to it,' 'no point to life at all?'* he pondered. He shook his head. *'Get on with it.'* He picked up a customer on the side of the road. He was glad to be driving, listening to crap. Some sameness, some deadening sameness!

Clem had been over in Mary's earlier. A pregnant Lorraine and her daughter Emily were down to visit mum. With Clem working nights and Emily up early, it suited that they met in the morning. Clem called at seven thirty.

Simon, Mary's partner, called down to move a tree that had blown over in the high wind.

"How's work?" Clem asked sat on the couch.

Simon gave a shrug. He's in the construction game, a bad place to be in this economy. "You know yourself."

"Hmmm!" Clem had forgotten. He'd a bit of money now. More than he'd ever had in his life. He'd stopped gambling and was saving away.

They played a little of the 'it's bad' game but Simon came from money, not too much but a bit. Mary, Clem's sister, had a good job in IT. They weren't doing too bad. Lorraine, Clem's other sister, wasn't having it easy and Clem would prefer to manage his P's & Q's. She was struggling but getting by. That's the effect it has socially. Groups of friends and families divided by current fiscal standings.

It was one of the main factors for their mother's depression in the eighties. It was why their father's behaviour lightened up in the nineties.

"There's a guy I know," Simon went on, "he's an electrician.

"I was pricing a job on the same site and his young fella was tending him. The young fella said to him, 'I don't know how you do this?' His old fella, who's been in the game for years said, 'there you are, take a hint from this, study your balls off in University and get a good job'."

There's that word again 'get a good job!' or the one he heard more often that really annoyed him, 'it's a job'. It irritated him beyond belief.

They'd a long discussion about the history of commerce. Simon referencing many things that Clem was intrigued about never having heard about. "The Japanese philosophy of 'restraint and create'."

"The black man says about the white man, that he'll come and stay and add to the place, 'watch out for the white man' they used say, 'because they're crazy! They're mad.'" Simon, mimicking the white man, puffed out his shoulders and head like a twenty-five-year-old at a disco, walking up and down to survey what was going on, wanting a piece of the action.

"The black man used to say about the Chinaman or Asian, they come in and do their trade and keep trading and when there was no more in it for them they'd head back to where they came from. They preferred even though he was 'crazy and cruel' the white man hanging around, building the place up and integrating."

"I'll have to check this stuff out, I'm doing research at the moment," Clem said. "Carry on."

"The white man is crazy, all over the world he's known as crazy. There was a guy, what's his name?..." Simon scratched his head. "He went looking for trading posts over by India, the gulf and down the back of Africa." Simon paused. "De Gama!". It sounded like a footballer's name. Clem was surprised, of course he'd heard of Vasco De Gama, but he'd thought he went to South America, *'maybe later'*, he really needed to learn a lot more about things.

"So he ended up in this place in India and the local traders didn't want anything to do with him. They brushed him off and sent him away from the port." Simon giggled a little. "This is how brutal the white man can get."

Clem had seen the movie 'The Mission' a few times, depicting the barbarism inflicted by the Spanish and Portuguese upon the indigenous populus in South America.

"So da Gama wasn't having any of this. These places had been around for years and years and years, all trading away between themselves. So he came back a few years later and blew the place to smithereens. He started pirating along the coast, if he wasn't having any of the action, then no one was getting it. The trade came to a standstill, no one wanted any dealings with this 'crazy white man'. A high priest was sent to negotiate with da Gama. Da Gama called him a spy, had his lips and ears cut off and a pair of dog's ears tied to his head and sent back to the chief."

Clem looked at him with great surprise. It was a surprise, but where was shock these days?

"Da Gama looted a ship with four hundred Muslim pilgrims on board, he sent them underdeck and set the ship on fire. He was seen looking through the porthole at them lifting up their babies begging for mercy."

"Humans are crap!!" Clem answered. "Well, not all humans… but why?"

Simon pursed his lips and shrugged his shoulders.

Clem had thought this many times. Why the terrible suffering of humans? Men, women, children. How exposed we all are to oncoming forces we cannot see. The priest might have suspected he might be in for a rough time with da Gama, the babies on the ship, depending on age, must have known little. The older ones the dread of impending doom. Were they, in their minds, going to be saved and go to heaven? As the pain of the fire lacerated their skin.

Dying can be painful. A lot of drugs Clem wants when he dies. A lot of morphine, he'd love as little pain as possible. He remembers he has to live first.

Clem checked it out on the internet and found himself looking up "what is an iso-static restraint," which he found out were statically definite restraints allowing you simply to support a body. "What the hell has this to do with life?"

"Is the roof caving in?" he asked himself.

'If people are spending a lifetime studying isostatic restraints and a lifetime studying organ transplant and air ambulance rescue drills... I guess I can see merits in that!!' he mused. He'd picked up an old man and his wife from the Oncology ward, an American. He gave his life story, which was about family and plastics. Clem thought, *'family fine, plastics hmmm?'* Years later dropping another customer to the airport he was telling Clem, "how the light reacting with the plastic wrapping of a tablet can change the molecular structure of the pill."

What has this to life? Yeah, it benefits humanity but Clem's life. Why was he looking up Hebrew, Hypnosis, Palmistry and now Iso-static restraints? How much, perhaps like Victor, did he really need to know? What did he need to know? Why would he go down this avenue? He wanted glory, fun and fairness. He guessed not everyone could have it, and as the years passed, that's what he was turning into, a number. Was he in a mid-life crisis or had he always been in one?

'Was love going to pass him by, like life?'

It was getting late in the day for Clem, whatever talents he possessed, if any, were fading or remained unutilised. Now, there was no heaven. Only a few days into the new year and things had a sour feel about them. Was he a possessed lunatic chasing Mariella? Was she giving him the run-around? The only good thing was August seventh was getting nearer.

He was trying to get to the centre of the make up a man. Himself, the full guinea pig. He was fine with being a doormat, it gave him a character to write about. It was more truth than fiction. His forty cigarettes and ten cups of coffee. Stagnated presence socially. He was a pariah, looking in. Looking in at the world, himself. He left the abstract nature of things, it's just the way it happened. And now, between the logical and illogical of reality lay the minefield of madness and depression. He'd have to fight every hour, every day. Just 'hang in there' as so many people do.

He researched a brief history of Vasco De Gama. It checked out.

Clem had a lot of people in and out of his taxi. Most were normal, plain, everyday, humdrum. People came out with stories they thought were exciting, that when Clem compared them to his own mad adventures or plights were quite dry. Clem had done a few wild things. He asked a friend, "how bad were they?" … "As to the everyday pieces of trouble? A bit on the wild side... more like *Leaving Las Vegas*, than *Fear and Loathing*." Clem accepted that.

Anytime he dropped someone off to "run in and get a CD," he couldn't fundamentally argue. Harder drugs hadn't been his thing, his was alcohol. He was glad with that. He enjoyed it more but he'd never know now, though those pills he'd taken in May gave him another idea, he was fairly glad it was alcohol.

There was one customer – only one! – who made him feel uncomfortable. He was glad to see the back of a lot them but only one stuck out. Clem realised he'd had him in the car before, the conversation was following a familiar thread but deeper, darker.

He got in, in the centre of town, with a girl.

"Where are you off to?" he asked as they reached simultaneously for the doors of Clem's taxi. One place geographically followed the other. He was a reasonably good-looking man, tall, both well-built and spoken. They agreed to share.

The customer started talking to the girl. Somethings were slipping during his conversation. A little neediness. Hints of resignation. Clem knew because at times he'd hear the same thing coming from his own mouth. This man's slips were more. The journey was brief enough, it was noticeable from the female passenger's return of conversation she was missing something too, a loneliness. Another night out on the town, yet again unfulfilled.

They talked about meeting up and swapped numbers. The reservations were starting to drip through to her, slowly, but her reality was she didn't need to heed them, not yet. They both got out of the car and spoke for about a minute. *'Is he going to score?'* slipped through Clem's mind. But no, he returned to the front seat. They had no sooner left that avenue, he'd discussed the girl a little, then he'd entered into a dark phase of conversation. Clem let him talk, Clem needed to know what goes through certain minds.

"I'm a manic depressive," the conversation reached quickly.

"I've tried to kill myself many times," he brushed back his sleeves to show the scars across his wrist.

"I've been in and out of institutions for ever, I'm not getting better, I'm never getting better!

"I've been thinking now… for a while, the best way to do it!" he continued.

"I've done the overdoses, the jumping, the wrists, rope…" Clem was really weary. His tone was dark, his head hung forward. Clem had had depressed people in the car before, his mind had travelled to the dark zone a few times but this was ridiculous. Clem had tried to interject, offer, empathise, the man could see Clem had some dealings with this, like a social worker but besides the man, the man and that dark place he was talking to just himself. Clem understood this, he was not going to upset anything, even the back of Clem's own mind knew to keep quiet, not a peep.

"Next right! I think I've figured it out," the customer continued.

"Seventh house down. Nitris oxide, you don't feel a thing, I'm going to get that soon!"

Clem could have tried, he'd help so many lost people, fed up people, what could he say to him?

"£16.45?" the customer asked.

"£15 is fine!!" Clem answered.

"Here's twenty. You don't do numbers, do ya?"

"Nah! If we meet again we meet again, that's my philosophy!"

"No problem, thanks."

Clem drove away, calmly. As if someone had given him life. There was something about that man that would stick forever. No one goes there, no one talks like that, no one walking the street, no one normal, maybe in sanitoriums or the like but they have, or are meant to have serious mental illness, a lot of the time genetic. But this was more, more, so much more. A joker, a wild card, a certificate of sanity for life. A return ticket to and from any dark or sad place in the mind Clem could ever wish to go!!

That's what this was, just a visit, a check-up, a service, anytime he felt it get dark or too dark he'd think of that journey. Strange how the customer's force, his misfortunate force would have such a positive one on Clem.

Clem wanted to run from the inside out. Grab the world and hug it, kiss it, make love to it! He realised he was 'in character'! talking a deep, profound game, waiting to figure things out. That's why he was going here, to the 'why are we here?' metaphorically 'checking his run up before the jump.' The last time he'd have 'his wet finger in the air' 'picking a few blades of grass and throwing them into the breeze'. He was for all intents and purposes making that jump.

Yeah, he'd slowed down over the last few weeks but the time was coming for that one great shove. It was okay, in the meantime to run with 'why are we here?', 'who's God?' Metaphysics, philosophy, nurture versus nature. Exploring the philosophers.

Chapter 19

Supper in Silence

Clem finished his shift on the fifth by dropping another atheist to the airport. A British republican, a well-meaning sort, of which he knew there were a sizeable proportion. Clem asked, "are people in Ireland still exhaustive about accents?" The response was a mild 'yes'. Clem felt when the 'strange accent' came to Ireland they generally had to be more yielding than the locals. Would he have to do the same in Spain?

He was giving a little too much to Clem, too easy. He went through the 'What he was doing' routine again. Clem returned a few out of decency. Granted it was five o' clock in the morning and the guy just wanted to get to the airport. The English guy had been on about the monarchy. Clem argued they're a tourist attraction. The man argued they shouldn't say anything. Clem argued, having already agreed they were generally on the same side of the spectrum, that they, as people in influential positions, were entitled to say something.

"They're not elected!" was his one argument.

"Neither is Alan Sugar nor Stephen Fry! As much as you'd disagree or agree with anyone in the public domain, that they have their say means only more people have to come forward and make a counter claim or agree. The rest of us generally suffer in silence."

Clem was asked in a club in Vigo once. Ireland was going through the start of austerity and a decent, intelligent, bearded young man, 'Welcome to Spain, would you like a free beard?' was how he summarised the attitude of the general Spanish male. This suited Clem as he was generally a shave-once-a-week man or if he'd nothing better to do.

Clem liked Vigo, he'd been there four times and made some great friends. It was his retreat. He'd always go back there, again and again. He remembers the last time leaving, the early days of January two thousand and ten, promising himself not to go back until he truly fixed himself. It was clear then to him. Something was missing, something wholesome, a part of him was wrong.

Yeah, he could fill it with love or could he even do that? What point would it be anyway? Really! Without clearing himself out? Without understanding? As he waited in that bar, he never liked, across the street for the overnight bus to Madrid to pull into the platform, he knew something had to be fixed. Something big, something great, something that he knew was in his mind or his heart or his soul. It was blocking him, plugging him, dragging him and he really couldn't be free until he set the snag loose.

It wasn't gambling, it wasn't alcohol, it wasn't mum, it wasn't dad, it wasn't the suppressive past of his country, it wasn't a system or an ideology, it wasn't scientific, it was Clem against Clem. The next time he'd arrive by whatever mode of transport and with whomever, he would be rid of it.

Clem had gone to the club come late bar. Full of good-looking women and beards. Clem assumed the character of being a millionaire so it would get the young man to think about who or what he might be addressing for future reference. The young man quickly got fed up. Clem thought of how one would have to adapt to people of different status. That though circumstances may change for a public. There would always be individuals whose perspective or complete understanding, weren't affected, or affected differently.

Don't write anyone off or in. *'Stop being a prick Clem!'* also crossed his mind. *'Yeah, why do you have to keep doing that?'* he gave out to himself. It wasn't Clem, really it wasn't him. He'd have to stop that. He'd become a crank. He heard himself, he was sounding more and more like Kate, 'there he went again', that wasn't Clem.

People's perceptions were there to be changed and learnt from. Challenged, rebuked and ceded to. Clem's mind was turning into an oasis, a sponge for open and diverse conversation. He was getting it from the public who entered and exited his world through the doors of the taxi. It had been a history and religion lecturer who had pointed him in the direction of John S. Scotus, the most famous philosopher of his time. Clem had delved into Socrates and Plato, right back to the birth of philosophy.

How relevant is this to a life? How much of a portion of this did he need to take on board? How relevant to his life? To leave questions behind. To find the answers he was looking for without spending the rest of his life looking for them. So he could live with a freedom that would no longer inhibit the true desires and wishes that were within his spectrum. To be rid of killing time with no more a purpose than to be killing more time. That a cause, distraction or fulfilment be found of true worth that would drape his life with colour and beauty. Like the million euros, but better.

He knew or felt that Madrid was not the answer but it was only a step away from it. He dreamed of a house in the countryside, more a studio, where people would get together to create art, share ideas, philosophise. He didn't intend it to be a commune, he wanted it to be commercial, viable, a retreat but with extending tentacles to the modern, to culture, to influence, to shape and infect in a bright manner.

If he made the money from the bar, he'd buy cheaply in the countryside, a finca or ranch. He'd hope to use the bar as a rendezvous, a source for interested parties and individuals. Uninstitutionalized, without becoming static and stale. Fresh vibrant people to continually flow through. It was a fantasy. He was lonely but still strong. Still vitriolic, still trying.

He'd drift off into websites for *Bares de alquiler*, *Bares para rentar*, mad, sweet happenings, his own manor, that's what he really wanted. He didn't trust people with too much of what he wanted to give. It had been wasted. He'd find a place where likeminded people met, with respect for each other. But that's the thing with humans. It's hard to keep everyone happy.

A chill out place where things could be done and analysed away from the speed of the Metropolis. Where life was slower, a little more relaxed.

Where writers, sculptors, painters, musicians, mathematicians could come together to formulate plans. Clem had been to the 'occupy protests' in Cork. What ideas in a modern world ran out of legs or steam without appropriate action. It was marketing and that's where he felt the 'occupy campaign' fell short. The modern world was so much about the 'me', according to the media, it wasn't true but it had sold itself thus. Clem guessed, *'isn't this about me?'*.

Clem was definitely going to sift some benefits. He was reared that way. It was his nature, his insecurities still had a presence inside. Clem always loved the 'few', 'very few', who seemed so happy, so at peace with themselves. He could feel their solace rub off on him. It was beautiful. Clem felt he wasn't far off them, just one step away.

Religious people were amazing this way. Full of conviction. Full of understanding, blind understanding. Like the pilgrims on the boat until an outside force of a De Gama interrupted. Was it necessary to change these people's minds? They were 'stoned' on religion. He'd enter into discussions with them. He never went too far with them.

One night as a passenger in a taxi, a Muslim with a fine healthy beard collected him. Clem had been done with Christianity and decided to pose the question. The driver talked a little about Mohammed, Clem interjected, and gave a little of his philosophy. "That we're all like little pods pushed forward from the history of time and bounce off each other in an uncoordinated way that due to the vastness of time seems coordinated… heaven is everything that has led to now, and is now. This conversation with you or anyone, though seemingly so trivial has a knock-on effect forever though we cease to exist." Clem let the information travel, "that everything prior to now, for example, someone who was good to your great grandfather, might have propelled him to do better things and someone who did bad would have had an adverse effect on you, even though it happened some hundred years ago,"

"No! Muhammed is the way!!" the driver answered.

"What if I'm a prophet?" Clem asked.

"Muhammed was the last prophet?"

"What do you mean?"

"Muhammed said he was the last prophet and there would be no more prophets after him."

'How fucking convenient!!' Clem disparagingly thought in his mind.

Clem spent four clicks on Scientology. Ron L. Hubbard. 'Are all religions just based on books?' he laughed to himself, 'Sure, I could do one of those.'

Once in work, in a 'Monty Pythonesque' way he picked up a small piece of limestone and declared 'this is the rock on which I will build my church,' he managed to hold on to it for a couple of days. Reaching into his big donkey jacket pocket and feeling it. 'Oh yeah, that's the rock' before getting back to whatever he was doing. The work was so boring down there, in the nursery.

When it was busy it was fine but when it was quiet it was quiet. There was so little to do. Just being there was hard but he was younger then. The weekends were full with drink, gambling, girls and football. There was company, friends.

He often felt hypersomnia talking to certain people. They just went on and on and on. The surprising thing was the amount of characters down there. It was a refuge, during the Celtic tiger for battered minds, a bit of a rehab centre, no one was unemployed. Except when it rained, then everyone did as little as they could.

Some worked away, it was in their nature or they were worried, some were skimming, monopolising overtime. People aren't dumb. If it upsets someone they'd kick up a fuss and get temporary compensation.

Clem was about to check out Hinduism. In the meantime he'd seen a video of Hitchens talking about the birth of Vishnu, that it came from the slit in the side of a woman. Hitchens went on to talk about how religion constantly persecuted the woman, and referred to the vagina as a bad reference point to anything.

Clem agreed, if it is unholy then it's easy to manipulate a mass and conjecture them to a guilt they have received by being born of a specific gender. Another 'original sin.' Clem's eye was caught by a video about Mother Teresa, Hitchens lambasted her. Clem liked Mother Teresa, then Hitchens went after Jesus! Clem wanted to say, "hold on a second!"

He'd made up his mind Jesus wasn't the son of God, though it could be a metaphor but at the very least he was a decent philosopher. Clem had accepted the Roman conversion was no more than a 'political choice' but *'Jesus Christ... surely a philosopher!!'*

Apparently not according to Hitchens. He'd come back to it like the Bush vs. WMD's and Bush vs. Jong, maybe Hitchens wasn't right on everything. It was his fundamental disagreement with Hitchens. Hitchens had argued vehemently against the persecution of thought by religionists, but Clem still believed if it existed in thought then it exists, even if it doesn't at all exist. So a God exists even if it doesn't exist. It is up to evolution, education and culture to show it doesn't exist or logically doesn't exist if unprovable.

So what credence to live by? Are we left looking at each other? And we don't know whether to hug or fight... *'let's promote the hug.'*

That's the thing! Mariella had given him chances. Three chances. She'd let it be known where she'd be on the Friday in Madrid! If he really wanted to meet her he knew where she was. She'd messaged him, between him getting on the plane in Dublin and off the plane in Madrid.

She didn't tell him where she was, but she knew he knew where she was. He knew she knew, but she knew he knew where she was. A dilemma? She hadn't invited him. It was a sports social. He could go but he'd be a dead man if he did. What freaky desperate weirdo does that? 'A real man!' maybe in the mind of Mariella but somehow he'd let her down.

She'd built him up to friends, the night he was coming, no show. What he'd have gained that night would have melted so quickly nothing would ever have come of it. They repaired the relationship over the next few months. He was going again in March but though he hadn't been gambling, his work ethic was awful.

When the push came for the trip, he didn't have enough. She'd agreed to meet him but he didn't have the money. Well, he actually did have money. £450 and he promised to spend it on the two of them if she wanted him to do it, but it was coming toward Car Test time again and he could feel the dread of renting again looming closer. He explained it to her, she understood. He knew then, as certain as the first time he'd laid eyes on her that she was meant to be his forever, that this opportunity would pass and he'd never meet her again. Was that all she was worth to him? Was it the £450 period? Yeah, he was a gambler naturally, $450 was fine, add in weekend earnings, possibly £250, never that it works out that way. He could have gone to seven. But not the dread of renting a car, not that hole, never that hole again.

The irony of life was compounded when he got done for two hundred and fifty euros for having a printer without a receipt. Clem gave her credit too, for when he declared on Facebook he was down to his last eleven euros, she didn't run off and desert him. Things would never be the same from March though, he'd messed up.

He'd managed a lot more off, than on, gambling at this stage. He'd taken up a different form of gambling. The gamble that life would get better for him with his ass parked on the couch at home sitting in front of the television. Was he depressed? Was he a dark lonely old sod? He exercised a bit to get in shape for his visit to Madrid. Ate healthily, got some moisturising lessons from his sister. He could use Mariella as a crutch but would that's all it would ever be? Something more fundamental missing.

Was that why he was alone? He'd met two beautiful girls in the last two years. Many a man would have given a limb to have a chance with. Clem wasn't budging, he wasn't through with himself yet. One girl he'd made an impression on straight away. She and a friend were off for a weekend to Amsterdam. The next time he picked them up, in the spring, she asked him to go away with them to a festival in two weeks. It was tempting but it didn't fit in around his schedule.

Clem had a busy schedule. It all revolved around a figment of his imagination. He'd no room, as gloriously tempting as she looked, sounded and her mere gentle desire to touch him seemed. 'Stop, Clem!' he'd love to just drop it. Leave it go, but there was something horrible holding him, nagging him.

He hated himself, in a sense, for holding back. He just wanted to go! He'd done it before, lots of times but it was always there, that thing, when he got back. The forty-four nights of drinking in a row, well he was a bit sloshed then. Clem was only twenty, that part of him hadn't completely manifested itself. He was too busy 'being' but it was, there in the background, a muffled buzz. When he walked somewhere, when he had to make up some excuse to get money. Lots of places, different times, different places.

Eating alone wasn't as exciting as it had been. It wasn't that bad. He'd been to a few fake dinners with women, some with notions, that he neither wanted to talk to or screw. He got over that lie early. He didn't know how it worked for other men, 'if you're a bore go home.' Clem was a bore too, worse if he was putting it on. Sometimes there was no chemistry.

This girl was nice though 'but the schedule!' in hindsight, not now, because he was still in some schedule, 'the plan' he knew, he'd regret it.

The other girl was all women. A regular waitress, they swapped stories and started forming a bond. She was stunning, kind personality, one of the sexiest voices on the planet, the kind you'd find from a lady in a James Bond movie. It had gone far enough. It was time to act.

This one wasn't really about a schedule. It was about diving in there for the taking or at least trying, this would last a while. He was weighing the benefits of the company and ready to accept that it probably meant he'd never get out of Ireland. A hypothetical relationship on the internet. He'd made himself a few stupid promises during the period Mariella and Clem knew each other, the worst thing was, they were to himself.

He chose Mariella, for whatever bundle of reasons he compressed together, he chose Mariella. Another long shot. He was always prepared to pay the price, he only ever needed a long shot to come in once. There were good days at home too, when a golf bet was closing in on coming up or after a period of reasoning he'd come up with another epiphanic moment.

Arm rises and fist pumps like the days in front of PlayStation or out near a green on the golf course. They'd built upon the fake reality, supplemented it. A lot of the time it seemed like the final one but it disappeared into the wilderness of his mind. Was he a bit of a monk? Monastic?

Could he do that in the midst of a town, in the midst of a job, in the midst of a gambling hall? Were they more intelligent than him? Maybe. But didn't Clem have the prevailing silence to enter his mind, he could hear it consciously, didn't he have the access to other signals of human thought as they passed in and out his taxi.

Real life, unmasked life, disguised life, raw life, blood and gore life? Hadn't he seen already from a young age, seen the wrong side of life, the 'nothing one can do about a situation' life, the powerlessness, perceived or real, that one is restricted to within the diameters of head to toe?

Whether or which, he was getting out of the monastic existence and riding a one-way party train to his death bed. He was really starting to have enough of this. He liked how Hitchens drank a bit, smoked a bit, whatever else he did. He died young but lived well, according to Clem. Of what he knew.

Chapter 20

I'm More Than a Number by at Least 4%

Mariella was gone. Period. He'd had enough. Clem had figured she was bordering on the psychotic, he knew he was bad enough without her dragging him into her pyre. His poetry book was in the design and production stage. The timing of it was rushed, pure revenge but he was reasonably satisfied with the contents, not all of it though. He'd go with it.

It was strange that the initial rage was not jealously led. The first time this had happened. He wanted to 'fix her' and 'fix her good'. He'd promised to send her a copy and already he was thinking of what to write on the greeting card that would be accompanying the book. He hated sending it but he would do so with bitterness.

Outside of that, in a week he'd be a published author. He thought on it for a while outside the mists of rage Mariella bound.

'Relevance!' it would give him relevance. 'The hardest thing to find in life is relevance'. The secret to everything had opened up in front of him. It was back, the word 'Relevance.' Even if the poems were complete shit, and success was limited to a few copies sold to a few friends and a reading or two, it mattered to him. His lifelong dream of being an author would be accomplished and due to a technicality over bar codes he would be published as opposed to being self-published, for what that was worth. He had a few hours to come up with a title. He knew the most appropriate title was "becoming a prick" or "in the middle of being a prick" but he'd change it.

Was that why family is sacred? It offers the easiest route to relevance? Clem for the first time tonight believed he would never get married. Or have kids. The attractions of flesh in the female form had diluted over time. He wasn't up to it. It wasn't his thing. He felt a little glum. He still offered a glazing look at the female form.

It was the anger of his father, just then, that had filtered through to him. A life completed but far from complete. The same of his mother. That society has it, that families have their great loves, trials and tribulations. That's what they're there for. Pockets of relevance.

Clem would never have that relevance. Turning up after work to a loving home. It seemed idyllic. It seemed pleasant, 'where it worked'. He'd enough experience himself to see it wasn't all roses in the garden. He'd seen enough men in his taxi experience the desperation of a wife lost. He'd seen women flaunting themselves, trying to redeem what time had taken. A lot of anger, fear, loneliness, misunderstanding. Men walked all over, women in dread, it went with every second person, with those who looked forward to or hated getting home. It just seemed the way of the world, of the time. Happiness, suffrage. Different people, different nights.

Clem had been het up all day and the tiny tingle of panic under his skin started to simmer. The repetitiveness was a dose. The fear had not dissipated. He was still every second cigarette off chain smoking and drinking coffee half as often. He was afraid, nervous, what if this wouldn't go away? Never? Follow him forever like a shadow.

He figured it hard to deprogramme himself in an instant. He was not comfortable yet. As he drove around the streets, generally a bad economic practice as a taxi driver, just to avoid being static. The cursed hours, killing time hours. Quietness killed him because he had to listen to himself, again.

He'd laid in the dark of his bed for a few hours smoking cigarettes, thinking about Mariella. She'd used him, she was the using kind. Walked all over him from the start. He knew this, he'd been there with others. This time it was special though because he'd been able to hang on long enough to her to make a dramatic change.

It was clear to him he didn't need her anymore. He'd crossed that threshold. He was going to Madrid and the thought of her was the thing that had dragged him to it.

He'd been on holidays there eighteen years before, again the result of a summer rendezvous. Along with his friends they'd been invited to meet up with some English language students. Clem went first to Milan on a wild goose chase to meet Valentina, again an impossible docket.

He got the train as soon as he landed. There was no answer at the other end of the one phone call he made at Linate airport. It suited him, he could run. He got to Stazione Centrale and boarded the train for Madrid. He arrived two days later announcing, "seen the world boy and every one in it," to Patrick in Chamartín station. He was glad to be in familiar company again.

It's the thing with true love for Clem, it only exists in fantasy or beyond. He'd over the years had beautiful, intelligent women he yearned and longed and willed to die for, beg him for love in the end and he'd just shrug his shoulders and walk away.

He needed her for a while, a medusa, a muse. Like his mother needing a 'magic bullet', his magic bullet was a woman that didn't exist, or a place or a wealth. He was a wanderer to nowhere.

Ilse, an Austrian woman, had made three trips to Ireland. They spent a weekend together. She'd a boyfriend. Clem knew the women he met were messed up about as much as him. He answered the phone call the second time and the third time he'd just refused to answer.

Mariella was a wanderer too. He'd asked her once, she refused to answer. She had no idea about things. And wanted things so bad and then didn't want them at all. He had a nickname for her physical weaknesses. Jaws, nose, chin, shoulders, breasts, she was short as an imp and tedious in her voice. He should never have told her he loved the way she made him jealous, she wrenched his heart many a time with that information. Clem liked to remain relatively honest with her, it was strange, but the pain made him feel alive, the anger, the hurt.

Mariella got extremely, viciously jealous too. Any time he chatted or left a comment with a certain Paloma, she would have a fit of rage. Deleting previous photos he liked, so he knew he was not without some power, but she was the dominant force of the relationship until now. She'd made the best use of technology and photoed well with her long blonde hair.

She rarely had it tied up and never short, one look at those jaws and chin had most men running. The rest of her was great though. Really sexy hair, good body, good ass, great cheeks, great smile and a mind that was lightening and as wicked as it was tender.

She was ahead of Clem. He might have had talent but she'd a lot more time. That is until now. Would things be really that different once he'd a collection done? The satisfaction grew as the time for their publication grew closer. He read the proofs for grammar mistakes he found after a little while they drew him in.

He tried to remain cold about it but they had a draw. He'd been nearly immune to them and didn't really want to read them again but there they were, pulling him in, as a reader. There's power in his words that he didn't realise, like a hypnosis, a drug, a lure. Something different, strange, far more attractive than a mere article.

But Clem was different to that guy, those guys. Different guises of him wrote different poems. Then they were gone. Those people, mindsets. Or were they? Did they line up in a queue, those different voices, to have their say?

He recognised some of them, the parts of his mind that would come to the tip of his pen and just piss off back to the back of his mind. Who was Clem now? Why such a breakdown of the mind? Why so compartmentalised? Why slow the roundabout down so much to examine each segment? How long more before he let sound and sight return, driving and talking take over again. Why did he still stay in this stream?

Clem drifted to thoughts of Mariella, then others, he'd been realising how much like her he'd been. He sighed a laugh, thinking to himself. It dawned on him.

In his heart he couldn't be bothered with people like this. He knew Mariella was the same but what was she supposed to do? Head off to a nunnery. She had to do her thing too. They connected on a level of innocent fantasy. Like Romeo and Juliet, that's all it was and the reality would probably be a lot different if that came to fruition.

He'd turned a blind eye to what she got up to. No more or less than any twenty-one, twenty-two, twenty-three, twenty-four-year-old got up to. She was getting older, already, it reflected in her photos posted from Miami. He thought there was a bit of a hangover involved, she'd looked great in the summer but she looked weary in Miami.

He'd promised, comparing her to Agneiska, a Polish girl Clem had become besotted with, that if Mariella asked he would stick. It was time, if it happened, simple as that. Agneiska was stunning. She looked more Spanish or Portuguese than Polish. Every guy chased her. She was fashionable, arty and again completely messed up in the head. This was something Clem knew he'd had no involvement when he came on the scene. He figured he didn't help Mariella's state one bit over the previous three years.

The day arrived when Agneiska asked to move in. He was a father figure to her, minder, friend, but he knew she was up to some game. She'd offered herself for the taking. Clem had a screwed-up head, he was investigating. She threatened him with marriage to someone else. She was going to head to Poland, he wouldn't bite. She'd again asked to move in with him when she got back from Poland, unmarried. Clem said, "no!"

At stages what he wouldn't have done to have these things present themselves. He just didn't want it. He just wasn't ready. He was fine for getting into terrible mischief but what he'd seen had been such a stark warning he was point blank stubbornly going to say no. He didn't want to wake up one day and say, "this is what I want to do with my life." He was scared of that. It was the thing that scared him most of all.

The guys, like him, who woke up and thought, *'what is my life for?'* Clem in that respect was grateful for his upbringing. It was a better education than any math, geography or English lesson. Some kids learn other things, like, ‘if you don’t earn enough money, you don’t eat,’ and others learn, ‘if you don’t do what everyone else does, then you’re out. And they are out!!’ That’s out for them, it’s what they’re brought up in, nothing else has value to them. Clem’s lesson was, ‘if you wake up some day and figure out what you want to do you better not have surrounded yourself in a whole pile of shit you can’t get out of’, the best lesson he’d ever learn?

Of course he could have been lucky and surrounded himself in glorious surroundings, a beautiful wife, great healthy kids but it’s hard to tell them one day, “you know, I think we should abandon this style of life because I’ve realised, actually I’m a little bit weird at heart and I’d like if we jumped up sticks, sell the house buy a ranch in the middle of Spain and turn it into a studio.”

There are two reasons a lot of that is false. He was only ever attracted to dreamy, arty types and they would be okay with that. But he was really in some perverse way only attracted to ‘horrible bitches’.

People get a lot of time to think in a lifetime. He agreed with himself to consider ‘a marriage of convenience’ if he got to forty still single. He really hadn’t considered it yet, maybe when he’s forty-one. If a woman needed a husband to look after and Clem needed the company, and the benefits were equally mutual, he saw no harm in that. It was totally against his romantic nature but elements of practicality might have taken over on both parties sides.

Clem also remembered twirling ‘the stem around the apple’ going through the alphabet to find the initial of the girl he was going to marry. Depending on the current occupier or potential occupier of his heart, would correlate with an exertion of effort approaching such letter.

And there was the sixteen boxes of course, four for number of children, four for wives' name, four for the year they'd get married, and four for the destination on their honeymoon. Clem smiled. He was also going to be a millionaire many times over by now or at least a million for Pete's sake. He giggled as he imagined the echo of the child in him giving out to him, "how couldn't you have a million by now?"

But he'd be 'a poet?' his old young self would have been fine with it but he could hear some more modern part of him, one of the material cheeky parts, next to the boy of him saying, "what good's it being a poet?" Clem laughed, all three laughed.

Clem needed dinner.

In this world of celebrity was he jumping a level? A tiny level. He wondered. He'd be a poet now. Now and forever, not to be taken away from him. What trappings go with that? Very little, he was at the bottom rung but still he was off the ground and the mass populous never get that high.

His sister had warned him about humility. It was something he had, generally, except for the attention-seeking part of him, but that was making up for a part of him that had never been satisfied. He was humble. Anytime he got praise, he shied away, though he sought it so much, when it was given he felt an extreme embarrassment. It was what he was naturally, a giver.

As much as he needed, he loved to give. He loved to give without it being known. His mouth betrayed acts of generosity sometimes, if enough time had elapsed he'd be fine and forget about it. He never really dwelled on things, Mariella, to her credit, was similar. They were both of the forgive-and-forget nature but when they went to war, they went to war. Now it wasn't about war. Clem had won but Mariella was winning, he'd put his little oar in now and twist a little pain, more so she could feel it. It was dessert.

As he drove, he thought of the book complete. The one he was writing wouldn't be complete until August, when he left. A lot of time on his hands. He thought about the music. He'd planned to make an E.P. sometime when he arrived in Madrid but now he decided to do it before he left. *'Might as well.'* Stephen was in a band, musician, singer and songwriter. He'd agreed to weigh in with Clem if he ever booked the studio. Clem thought of the few photographs he took. *'I'll do a book of those as well.'*

'What good is it being a poet?' that really bugged him. Poetry is nothing, no money in it, no glory, no fame. It was a thing he always wanted to do but in society it gravitated such a short distance. Thought of, remembered, forgotten. Lost away on a shelf. What was in it? What great personal achievement was in this at all? It wasn't going to get him money or ass. He'd still have to drive next week. *'What good is it being a poet? What good is it tarring roads?'* he thought driving out the gate of his house, *'people drive on roads,'* he answered. *'What good is there in making cars?'* he asked *'People drive cars,'* he answered. *'Shut up'*… *'People read poems!'* …*'That's no good really!'* It's like PlayStation or golf or any non entity anywhere.

He was odd with himself. He didn't want to hear it. He just wanted some coffee and cigarettes. Just bind him to the circle again for a while. The bar in Madrid was really all that mattered. Any old bar. Anything that made a bit of money. A sing song, conversation, drift away from all these subjects. He'd dread if the 'sameness' followed him. That’s why he was doing this crap, to be rid of the sameness.

Chapter 21

It's All God's Fault!!

The next two days were seminal. Kate had broken up with another man, he didn't last long. He was developing a pattern similar to another guy and she just knew in the long run that it wasn't going to work. She wanted to keep it quiet. She'd been quoting references from a book all week about disfunction and function. Clem tried in ways to point out that the whole thing is a 'functioning disfunction, or a disfunctioning function.'

Clem didn't have a degree, so it bore no mass with Kate. She did give him some kudos though, Clem had done bright things before but often he just talked himself into holes. Kate was giving out about everyone. Clem knew she was doing it about him too. Word gets round. Clem was doing it to Kate, he couldn't stop himself when he got the loan of an ear. The two of them were frauds, to themselves, they were more honest in fighting each other than anywhere else but they kept their thoughts confined behind their lips most of the time.

This woman was cliché queen. The one that irked Clem the most was, "you only get out of it, what you put in to it!" Tell that to a man stuck behind a Yak for six months and a flood wipes everything he does out. Clem agreed 'you', 'he', 'one' has to work for things one wanted, that doesn't guarantee anything! So if someone is partying away having fun and someone is working to the bone and a big 'disaster' strikes them both at the same time, who wins? That's the hand he was dealt. He wasn't afraid of work. He was afraid of doing 'pointless work', pointless to him, Clem, work. What's the use in putting a whole lot of energy and time into something and walking into something and thinking or feeling or just right knowing, *'this isn't actually what I want to do at all'* and because 'people are looking' the main reason to continue doing it.

People are strange. Is it just Irish people? He'd been off as mad as a hatter for the longest time, on about stuff but people had been very kind, supportive. He couldn't tell the actors from the real ones, but most seem genuine. Then there were the customers that remembered him.

"You're the crazy guy who's going to…"

"What have I done now?" Clem would answer with a laugh but he'd been on the same line, same character so long now it was easy to keep to the story.

"I believe there's something about you. The moment I met you I knew there was something different about you… You're actually going to do something, I feel it."

It gave him a reluctant confidence, Clem believed it, well he mostly did, 'What else was there to do anyway?' He went along with it and fed the monster, his own monster! If he'd convinced others he must have convinced himself too.

Sometimes people cross a finish line and just carry on. Some, because they want to carry on to the next one. Others because they just can't stop. They can't look up. Look around them. Sometimes they can't stop because they've over programmed themselves so much that they don't know how to. Like Clem with the gambling, hiding time was over but it had taken him so long to stop that he'd lost another few years just pulling to a halt.

It was strange in a way. Both had preconceived ideas about the other. When he'd leave on Saturday the ashtray would be the first thing back in the sitting room. Kate had kept a lid on her anger. She wasn't in as strong a place as usual, what, with the break-up. The only thing was, she was still mantrafied. Clem realised he'd been the same. Kate had wanted change from within, Clem wanted his surroundings changed. He found it hard to see Kate changing. He could see how clearly implementing the effects of change on oneself were manifesting in the self. Did he really need such a radical change in his life?

"Three times the girl had to find out whether the ticket was okay, what's the story with that?"

"Maybe personally she wanted to give it to you but management might be prying their noses down on things at the moment."

'For a guy driving a taxi he makes sense sometimes. Far beyond most. He should have gone to University. What a waster. He could have a Master or a PHD. There he is driving a taxi, that he keeps in wretched condition. He hates me.

'Why doesn't he wash himself? Or take care of the house better? He'll have near enough on the same pants on for the time I'm here. He knows I'm catching him for a lift. I really don't want to deal with him right now. I've my own life to live, I don't know what the hell he's up to. Waste of talent.'

"You asked me to call you between eight and half past," Clem tapped on the door.

"Thanks Clem, what time is it?" Kate asked.

"Quarter past eight."

As he drove around that night. Again in the quiet spots, examining himself. He started realising he was what he was. A function of everything that had gone before. He started to realise he was 'a little different', maybe 'a little weird', 'a little dysfunctional', 'a bit abstract'. His thing in life was to create. He could work shit jobs and fall in and out of love over and over again. He might be totally delusional. He was suddenly becoming really, really okay with that. It's his thing. A 'hopeless loser'. Melancholic. Maybe to others but to himself he was really starting to like it. 'The guy who got away' or, 'Thank Christ I didn't end up with that nut'. He wouldn't end up that guy who does nothing and lives on his own. The one, the neighbours never figure out anything about.

Kate quoted Clem. From times gone by. "You said." It really never bothered Clem what he said, if it did he'd never go back to certain places or look a lot of people in the eye again. He smiled inwardly, which broke through on his lips. He saw himself, going around to people and saying to Eric in the garage, "remember I told you I'd make an album one day, well I never did it." Or the regular teacher passenger, "remember I told you I was going to Buenos Aires in two thousand and ten, well it's nearly two thousand and twelve now and I never did it." Or to Des, "When I'm rich from the stocks, I'm going to buy a football club and I want you to be the manager…well I never done it."

He could go on like that for so long about so many things, bands, books, records, becoming a pilot, in a rare way he was proud of himself. They had all been right about him, 'what a loser' he turned out to be. Wasn't it truly great to be 'a loser'? A victory would be nice but that would spoil it. He'd end up a 'crazy' man. An 'I can't believe he done it!' man. He would always be 'a really nice but doesn't give a shit' man. Clem needed to change! He needed to stop changing himself. He needed to change certain things around himself. He'd realised what a happy man he was. Happy as a melancholic man could be. It was what he was and he should be so happy about it, accept himself, love himself. He always did until he went away trying to change. For what, to fit in? Fit in, in a way that wasn't him. That wasn't Clem, that was never Clem.

He was lucky, so so lucky, cleaning wasn't his thing. Scruffy a bit, but more like rough-clean. He was the same with garden but even worse, and the carpet and the house. He wasn't a *Chicken Lickin'* 'the sky is going to fall down' type, generally. The sky was going to fall down in its own time. Nothing Clem was ever going to do was really going to have too much of a hand in that.

It was wonderful. It was freedom. What was the need to change? He'd enough of Ireland, Cork, taxi driving, he was still going to walk away. It was what he was. It was what he'd morphed into. He was bethrothen to anything. Any social norm that would suffocate him. He was there to question it, get others to question it. It was why he was here? He was, is here, to be a little weird! A dreamer.

All this time, it was starting to edge toward the front of Clem's mind. A man who'd back the three-legged horse, a man who somehow believed something would come along and intervene from the heavens. He realised his folly. God wasn't going to make that ball roll into the cup. God wasn't necessarily going to print the winning numbers on his lottery ticket. God was never going to make Mariella jump out from Facebook and be there ready to kiss.

God wasn't going to appear from nowhere and save him. He never was going to, he never will. Others might, family might but it wasn't God, it was people. God wasn't in him the night he picked up a man flat on the floor having a heart attack, the Devil wasn't in him the time he took money from someone's drawer. It was him, all him, Clem. God was redundant.

God wasn't looking at him praying, how to join his hands properly. The right way to bless himself. "This is the Roman way, don't do it like them or you'll be Orthodox." His destiny was always in his own hands and in the hands of others. Strangers. The time the guy gave him a day pass for the London underground. Clem didn't even know how it worked, he learnt quickly and it was ultimately the way to his Aunt's and refuge.

That wasn't God, that was a guy doing a simple random kind thing, it wasn't a huge thing. He could have as easily thrown it on the ground.

God wasn't in the casino ready to change his life with a result. Neither was he inside him pushing him there or dragging him away from there. That was Clem, which had grown that myth inside him. He was perchancing things to luck. The house has about a fifteen percent advantage on average. You bet a hundred euros you get eighty-five back. You bet the eighty-five and you get a continuing diminishing return.

That wouldn't mean some people wouldn't win big. That's a volume rule. One out of every so many thousand, hundreds of thousands, millions would win. It was an odds thing. The bigger the jackpot, the smaller amount of winners. Clem applied it immediately to love. He'd done it before. There will always be Romeo and Juliet stories but it takes a Romeo and a Juliet. So was Clem still prepared to be a Romeo? He was definitely going to remain romantic. He liked big odds, on less things though.

"God is everywhere? God is nowhere!" Clem said angrily. God doesn't exist. He doesn't exist in me. The thing all his life that was in him was God! A fallacy. A complete lie.

The echoes continued, it was no use, from here they'd only get fainter, weaker. He prodded out an ear to hear a few words as they slipped away. 'In the name of the Father, Son and Holy Ghost,'

"In the name of God man!!", "God sent you!", "God being good!", "With God's luck!", "If you saw God you'd be dead!"… "What a crock!!" Clem was rid.

There was no immediate lift for Clem. No sudden relief. That thing inside him, he carried around, his spirit, his soul was non-existent. It was others who shaped his life. So many of them had carried the spectre of God with them. Of not knowing nor understanding. Yet, like the reluctant serviceman, they give and take as knowingly as they have done blindly. As Clem has done, all his life. So why are we here? Clem asked himself. He knew, like he'd done with so many equations he inverted this one, it fit. Could he have really solved it? The meaning of life? Why are we here?

That 'thing' would go away now, this was his 'man thing!' the same as his father decided to go for a pint instead of going to the church. This was Clem's ultimate challenge, had he beaten Dante's inferno?

Chapter 22

Jay Kennedy

What Would Have Happened If Barabbas Had Been Up for Crucifixion a Week Later?

Cork was bringing him back to his old self. If he stayed here, he'd be worse than ever soon enough.

Clem dropped a few guys to Minane bridge, it ended up being a fair distance beyond. They were discussing a few things along the general lines of blaming society and life.

They were on about winning the lotto. Clem said if he won he'd buy a football club. The man in the back seat said, 'that's one sure way of losing money'.

Clem answered, "what's the point of winning it, if you're afraid of losing it?... stay at home just counting it."

The new year was in, the lads were fine. The guy in the front seat was off to sea tomorrow with the merchant navy.

"Do you ever just want to be in the middle of a fight? With machine guns an' stuff? The open sea, pirates... there must be strange stuff happen out there," Clem asked. He was drifting, dreaming, it was enjoyable.

"Strange isn't the word for it," the customer replied.

"There's a General who once he gets on land stays drunk for three months straight. I'll have 'the rats' again on board the first few days."

"I miss that, dude, I miss being wasted, it's been so long." At that moment he did. It seemed everything was happening for everyone else, Clem knew the truth of it, he'd learned from years of 'what'll happen without me' and 'what will I miss?' it didn't matter, he wasn't there.

It had been time, finally, for Clem to be studious, disciplined, industrious but at times he wanted to let go, break out, live. Some voice in the back of his mind was still around, the disciplined voice. Tonight he'd let him talk but not run.

"So the ship has a crew for the first few weeks dying with a hangover?" Clem asked eagerly.

"Yeah, everyone will be looking at each other with 'the DTs' for about two weeks."

"Wow! I love the whole fuckeduppedness of it all." Clem was there in his minds, sick, fat, sweaty stomach, how he missed it. How controlled his drinking had become, how sensible in many ways he was turning. Was he getting old?

"Strange stuff happens on the sea."

"I wrote a poem about that."

As fun a conversation as it had been, Clem forgot about the conversation as soon as the second man got out. He knew the area well, he'd brought mother down there on many a Saturday spin, he wasn't so great in the dark. He had to look out for 'a right' and 'a right' on the way back. He got lost down here before, between her constant questions and his ability to drift off to dreamland. Often he ended up on the completely wrong road. It was a price he'd have paid double for.

Clem enjoyed driving, most of the time. Not traffic, not queueing, driving. In his own mind he'd be anything, anywhere in no time. A sum might enter his head relating to any particular thing and in the back of his mind he'd start half laughing at himself. But the road would fall away nicely and whatever character he wanted to be he could delve into. He would belong to the canvass of the sky. He loved the exclusivity.

He was back in town. Did a loop of the main thoroughfare. His first ride involved dropping off a policeman to about as near as possible enough to the spot where he'd been flagged down. He'd been panicking about the time, about being late for work.

A different guy was collecting him to the one who collected regularly on a Sunday. He collected him every other day of the week but not on Sundays. This Sunday he was.

"You can't be phoning a guy at five thirty in the morning." Clem's car was a wreck now and the orange petrol light was glowing again. The brakes started to screech while driving. The tyres on the left were nearly balding, the back right mounting was rattling like a baby's prattle and the dirt both inside and out was putrid. Hard, dry bird shit, stuck on the back right door. It was really time Clem cared a little more. This was a taxi after all.

As he drove around a corner, he passed a customer he'd dropped, walking back from the train station. Clem flashed him but it was dark and the customer didn't see him. His friend or relative was off to Turkey, then Damascus, then Baghdad. Damascus was in Syria, Clem found out after asking. The thought of that put Clem's 'questions' into perspective. He thought of the 'my Daddy didn't hug me enough' hypothesis.

They were giving out about the governments and regimens and armies in North Africa. Clem didn't know the full situation, "It's always the people that suffer." He thought what 'great way forward' is there?' he needed to come up with something.

He dropped a regular couple, one to work at a hotel followed by dropping her boyfriend off home. As he queued outside the apartment complex a billboard reading, 'repent or thou will perish' faced Clem. It pissed him off. He felt like going over and writing on it, 'bullshit,' or thought on the journey in, 'what happened to the good Samaritan?' Or 'what would have happened if Barabbas had been crucified a week later?'

He hadn't given up on the whole search for 'why he was here?'. He'd become easier about it. When he'd let it sink in, it would sink in. It wasn't full closer, sure he'd gotten as much as he was ever going to get out of it, but shouldn't he dig a little more? Was he really close to the answer that has haunted the human race since its first awareness of the question? He was still near enough to the dark matter in his mind. It hadn't been put away like it was so often. All those times, during queues, gambling bouts, drinking binges. He could still give a glimpse. He'd the wild card to come back.

It had been earlier in the evening though. A comment. As he'd reached the top of the rank.

"John street"

"Ok!"

Going northside was tougher, hills, lights, tighter turns, the chicanes through town. A variety of customers were lined to get in. Two potential customers passed by over the dirt on his car.

"You're wrecked?" Clem asked the obvious question.

"Yip," he answered with his foreign accent, drunk following an exhaustive period of work. They're never that drunk, it only takes a few drinks to topple them over.

Clem took a chance on a late light. He got most of the way across the junction, but his rear was a little prone in a yellow box junction. A police car was hanging a right.

He'd seen taxis pulled for it before. Nothing. He drove on, little chat. He dropped him at his apartment complex, a tight, long little road. It climbed at the end. His window was down as he'd lit another cigarette. He'd have to pause as the road joined the bigger one at the T-junction.

Two girls crossed in front of him. They were saying something to a guy who was coming from the left, not far away. Clem could feel no great tension in what they were saying, neither a huge deal of affection. Last attempt at a one-night stand. It was just when the guy said, "I've come a long way to get here," and it immediately clicked with Clem. The journey from the sea, the beginning of time. Sperm. Egg. Him. Us. Everyone.

Less than a month later it all clicked. Mother had been dead sixteen days. Clem had tried to enter the mind of a killer, euthanasia. He couldn't do it. For all the repeating she was his mother. It wasn't his place to decide. He wanted her to die, to be rid of suffering but it wasn't his decision.

He'd needed a snag for his book. That's how the formula worked. A minor climax a third the way through. It was the perfect hook but it was half baked, a pup. He'd never have done it. It wasn't what he was here to do. Another whoreocrat to commercialism.

His mother's death brought a huge comfort to him. He drank solid for four days sticking respectfully to the protocol of a catholic funeral. 'High' from the end to her suffering. They, the family, had stuck with her. Seen her last puff of breath. For those that sympathised, that knew, that understood, Clem felt a strong unspoken bond. Only the experience that can teach.

The loss of her touched Clem deeply. The privilege of loss. No blaming, an easy acceptance. He loved the humility of it. It was the greatest feeling ever. To be humbled so beautifully.

He watched her die, lie in the coffin, driven to the graveyard and placed in the hole. He knew as he looked into the grave, before they dropped her down, he would never see her again. 'There's no coming out of there,' he accepted. He came back to the grave two days later to confirm it in his mind. The half wet turned over sods covered the hole. Done.

The urge to visit her alive came and went. The wish for kind memories hadn't visited him yet. He was impressed by the community's show of sympathy. He could see it working in a new format.

The poems were out a week before she died. He secured a profound sense of fulfilment. He sent Mariella a copy the day after. He was still confused by her implied response, he wasn't worried anymore, though he still looked at her profile. It half changed him.

Three days before her death he'd promised to stop writing. It was finished, only bits remained. The day before her death he'd come upon the 'meaning of life'.

He manufactured in his mind the conversation with Patrick after her funeral.

"I've discovered the meaning of life Patrick, why we are here. It was always going to be an obvious answer!!"

"What is it?"

"Buy the book, Patrick…"

"Ah, go on tell me!"

"We're here… to be human!"

Patrick giggled, thought it through for a few seconds, his eyes started to open to the simplistic realisation of it.

"What is human?"

Clem jumped in. "Human is, what human does." Clem paused. "And everything that happens to one!"

"What does that mean?" Patrick asked.

"Since we don't choose to be born or generally choose to die, we're here to be taken advantage off." They giggled. "…Really, it means do stuff, Patrick."

"Like?"

"Like save as much money as I can and head to Madrid," Clem answered.

The conversation never materialised. It would take a job two weeks later to confirm it. He had refined the concept a little and felt he had it perfect now.

"Hiya, taxi across the road… when you're ready," Clem said on the phone to the customer.

"No problem, a few seconds," he answered.

It was quarter to five in the morning. Clem guessed he'd be hungover or… his thought process stopped as he gazed out through the window, another decision had been made.

The customer was prompt and jumped in the front seat next to Clem.

"Where are you off to?" Clem asked.

"Lee road," the customer answered. About a ten-minute trip. Clem gathered his thoughts as to the cheapest route for the customer. He'd got it.

"How's your night?" Clem asked. The question nicely paced in keeping with the time of the morning.

"Good," he replied. Pleasant tone. No signs of too much drink.

"I was watching a show about a guy who has lung cancer… it's a series! The first episode of six," he answered at a somber pace. "It's about what he's going through, about life."

Clem's lower mouth dropped half puffing a relief.

"Is he young?" Clem asked.

"About middle aged," the customer answered. "It gets you thinking about the whole thing… life."

"I'm doing the same," Clem responded. "Not the lung cancer, touch wood," tipping the staring wheel as he said it. "I've been looking for the meaning of life for month… years," he said with a gentle flail of his hand. "…Maybe twenty or thirty… all my life."

Clem asked him to open to the glove box where his poetry book was. The first poem was about a woman who had cancer Clem had in the taxi once, just coincidence Clem accepted.

"I've been asking questions," Jay responded.

"I know the meaning of life," Clem claimed. A hush followed.

"Go on!" Jay asked facing Clem, awaiting, knowing he was going to get an answer.

"Buy the book," Clem answered. He was hesitant, it was a secret he'd have to give away. Once it was gone, it was gone.

Jay looked at him. He understood. Clem understood too. 'Try it!' Clem thought.

"To be human!" Clem answered.

Jay paused to consider the information in his mind. He wanted more.

"It was always going to be obvious," Clem added. A silence again lingered.

"I am a man of science," Jay declared. "I am of the same thinking."

"Philosophy is the middle of math and language… there is a lot of science in the English language."

"What is that so?"

"For the species… survival, for the individual somewhere between 'what one is capable of and what an individual wants.' For me it's 'to make things better.'"

"So, it's somewhere between what we can do and what we want to do..." Jay intervened.

"It's about finding what's right for oneself!" Clem finished.

Jay took his time considering. "I get it!" He was intrigued and quietly moved. Clem saw it, affirmation. His theory was right. "I changed can for capable... it's a better word." Again Jay acknowledged.

Clem went through his theories. Time plus energy equals life. That time was a loop and on.

Jay said he was interested in the future, sci-fi. "They put it out there." Clem gave him his theory on one day humans leaving the planet. Jay knew all this. Jay came back with human genetic modification, the improvement of the species, he was turning out to be very knowledgeable.

Clem answered his individual future was in a box in the ground and because he'd discovered 'the meaning of life', he had contributed more than enough to the human species. Jay shook his head and nodded in agreement. He said he'd keep an eye out for his book. He shook Clem's hand again. It was congratulations. Clem was humbled and awed. Affirmation from an intelligent man, it was everything he could wish for.

He'd made the decision a day earlier that he was going to Madrid in May. The stock market had rallied from the day his mother died, again only coincidence from Clem's view, he was amused by the irony. New taxi regulations meant renting a taxi for the last ten weeks was illegal. No symbolism. His car test was due by May. It was time to go. He was happy.

A week later as he smoked another cigarette and drunk another cup of coffee alone in the dark curtain drawn living room, a great pain came across his chest. His face started turning blue and his breathing incredibly restricted. Clem was suffering a heart attack.

Chapter 23

The light had been strengthening toward dawn. The bare trees were beautiful without being majestic as he drove towards home. *'Familiar roads,'* Clem thought to himself. He pulled into the local supermarket carpark and started jotting down some thoughts for the end, was it going to end so limply, so sadly.

As he wrote, a tap on the window.

"Would you take me to the city?" the man asked as he opened the door.

"Sure…" Clem answered. He'd seen him at the entrance on a mobile phone as he entered the carpark. Clem thought he could have 'knacked' him if he'd tried but he wasn't in the mood for it, neither was above it either.

"Where am I?" he asked

"Togher, or The Lough, if you want."

"I don't know Togher or The Lough… I'm from Fermoy!"

Clem was still happy, he repeated the question, Clem answered the same.

"I was at a party in Douglas, I don't know how I ended up here. The Guards were called an' all."

Clem would have given a response but this customer was the conductor of this conversation.

"I had to get my mobile, they threw me out because it became… too much drink and stuff. They wouldn't let me back in to get my mobile, so I went next door. I knocked at the door and the Guards were called.

"Where are we at all?"

"The Lough," Clem answered as they passed the lake he walked by many times on the way to school.

"I just wanna get out of here. I just want to get out of the city," the customer continued.

"We'll have you there in no time." Clem was smiling.

"I'd never have walked this. Was I telling you the guard came along... well she was a right bitch! 'I'd like to speak to your commanding officer.'

"'What are you doing at these people's property at this hour of the morning?'

"'Well, they won't let me get my mobile back.'

"She got it back for me anyway… Is that the right time? Half five," the customer continued unrelenting.

"No, quarter to nine," Clem responded.

"Yeah, I'm glad to be getting out of here. You're born, you live, you die."

"Hmmm!" Clem offered.

"You're born, you live, you die! We're going to a better place after this surely!"

Clem shrugged his shoulders. He knew different.

"I've seen a lot," the customer went on. "I'm as gay as they come. Life's a party. Grab life by the balls."

"The bus station, thank God. Can I have your number?"

Clem scuffled around, there was one card. Clem didn't do numbers generally. Something was already written on it. He put it back.

"In case I need your taxi services if I'm back in Cork. What's your name?"

"Clem!"

"Okay, take care, man."

"Thanks. You too, man," Clem said cheerily.

Clem sang a little as he drove off. As he passed through the town's streets, back toward the shopping centre, he wandered off into thought. He wasn't going to find company, here, in his new world. Poignancy was dead, nothing even to symbolise anything, as he passed by his secondary school. Nothing holding on to him.

He slowed down at the entrance to the supermarket and indicated in. It was Sunday morning. *'There's Dennis, heading for the recycling bin,'* he paused in thought. He was about to criticise Dennis by saying, "doing the same old shit as always," but he liked Dennis. *'He's alright,'* the stream ended. Clem had no problems with Dennis.

He'd feared him for a long time growing up. It was his daughter that had caught him stealing the biscuits. Dennis and Clem had built up a rapport over the last five years. Soccer was the common bond but they never talked on the subject.

Sat in the carpark, appraising everything. It was quiet around. He was going to be sad, eventually depressed. "Have I been depressed all along?" He didn't know but it was the only obvious place left for him to go.

Clem walked down the aisle and picked up a loaf of bread that he wasn't sure whether he really liked. If it was the right one, he loved it. If it was the wrong one, it was like 'plaster'. He went for a small slice pan, he was surer he liked that, even if it wasn't his favourite. He headed back up the aisle, to the fridge with the special offers. Three euros for peppered burger steaks or four pork chops, reduced.

Clem picked up the burgers. Dennis was facing him but fully involved in a discussion with someone by the newspaper stand. Denis, shifted a little, temporarily leaving the discussion with whoever's back was facing Clem.

"Hiya, Clem!" Dennis acknowledged.

"Hiya, Den-ni-s." Clem answered positively as he was walked by.

He paid for his food and checked his lotto numbers underneath the scanner. Clem didn't know how to use it so he had to slow down to read the instruction. It scanned.

'Not A Winner.'

It didn't take Clem long to figure it out. It was the greatest moment of his life. Dennis, with a simple but earnest kind effort, had sent forward, to Clem, a whole new equation.

Clem wanted to write but he was tired. He went to bed. He slept for three hours. He dreamed. It was the first time he'd dreamed of his father in nearly four years. It was the first time they didn't argue. It was the first time Clem hadn't told him, "fuck off". In his dream his father started agreeing with him, encouraging him. Clem rushed from bed at one.

The sun shone through the window. He didn't check anything with Mariella, he went downstairs, had cigarettes and coffee and started to write.

Three days later his poetry book would be in his hands. He'd drive down to Patrick and give him the first copy. He always said he would. He went to the post office and would send Mariella a copy. He'd add, 'I managed to keep one promise (if it reaches you).'

He called up to mum to cheer her up. He stayed the forty minutes, by the time he was finished he was in dire need of another equation. None came forth, so he relied on previous ones. He went home to bed and got up early in the morning. He wrote all morning, glad he didn't flick it, glad that he was an equation with the sense to wait for Spain. Glad that he loved her.

He got called into work early, he had been sleeping and the base was busy. He was extremely fine with himself. Something had changed. It was quiet around, damp, drizzly, queueing he headed off the queue and drove a few miles. He was fine with it. Queueing around wasn't his thing, *'so drive,'* he was smiling to himself. He got five jobs in the four hours. He was late on the third job. He'd squeezed in 'a quickie' from when he'd got the job over the radio and then got lost counting the numbers in the estate.

He found them, twenty minutes late but the customers were having a social evening. They were in their thirties and headed for the western suburbs of the town.

"I know."

"Your father's been through a lot with his heart problems."

"I know."

"My brother now, he finds it nearly impossible to walk across the road. It takes a monumental effort to do it."

The second girl nodded in approval.

"It must be so hard for your father, with the cardiographs and tablets he has to be on for the rest of his life."

"It's a huge surgery!" the other girl answered back.

"I'm sorry girls," Clem interjected, "but did you ever hear of those people who faint when people talk about blood and guts and whatever, I'm one of those," he told in a sweet tone.

"But we weren't talking too much about blood and guts," the lady behind his left shoulder claimed.

"No, just in case you did," Clem said softly. "Like a sympathy vomiter?" he added.

"I've heard of them alright," the girl directly behind him answered.

"How come?" they asked simultaneously.

"I guess, sometimes I imagine it further on, more blood, tubes and sometimes very rarely I'd faint…" he didn't want to say it but he did, "I'm a writer…" he said confessionally. "We imagine things on and on and..."

"Oh really?" they asked.

"What do you write?'

"Poems and a philosophy novel."

"And have you anything written?"

"Well, I've… the poems are out a few days."

"Can you tell us one?"

He'd done this an odd time in his taxi career but it was getting old for him now. He'd never learned 'off by heart' anything since he was younger and he'd have to think hard to remember.

He was getting ready. Scanning in his mind a poem he could remember as he looked around he spotted the proofs between the handbrake and his seat. He picked up the proofs.

"Are ye able to read?" he realised they were sober but fairly tired.

"Yeah, sure... hand them over," they said.

"Which one?" Clem fiddled with the steering wheel as he tried to pick out one of two.

"One of your favourites?"

Clem knew two that got good receptions, that were safe but a favourite. It was like picking a child.

Clem turned on the rearview light and handed over the proofs.

"Pick them randomly," he suggested.

There was silence as the girls went reading. Clem saw they started on the back one, *'a good one to start.'*

The pages slid.

"Did you get lessons to write like this?" the girl on the left asked.

"No," he said half dismissively.

"I'm not really into poetry," she said after a little pause.

"It's not really her thing but I am," said her friend. "Remember I bought that poetry book." She was still reading.

"What's the book about," the girl on the left asked.

"It's about, why are we here?… or why am I here?" Clem answered.

"Why are we here so?" the girl on the left asked.

"Buy the book."

"Come on tell us."

"Ah, never mind," Clem said

"Ah, go on tell us," the girl on the left urged.

"Because this is heaven!" Clem responded calmly but with resonance.

"That's me screwed," she answered flippantly, her smiling interested face dimming a little.

"Heaven isn't a place we're going to," Clem interjected with a swing of his hands skywards.

"Heaven is here, here and now, there's no point changing yourself for the sake of it or for someone else, you've heard of the saying 'the grass is always greener' well sometimes… it is! And if ain't happening for ya here then find where it is happening for you. Or who it is, or what it is."

"You're a bit weird."

"Seven billion gods trying to be human."

She cheered up, smiled again, peaceful.

The other girl continued reading. The girl on the left got out just before the bridge. A turnaround and off up the hill to drop the last girl home.

"Do you really get faint?" she asked.

"A rare time."

"When can I buy this?" she continued.

"Next week."

"I'm going to buy a copy," she claimed.

"Really?" Clem exclaimed in surprise. "Why?" he asked.

"I met the author and I like it, the first five are a bit morbid though."

"Yeah, when I was checking them I was glad to just slip through them. It's strange, even as a proofreader, after being a writer, then a reader, how the words just draw you in for a while, take you away," Clem declared.

"Yeah, that's all you really want."

She read some more as he spoke softly to her.

"Left here, yeah?" Clem asked.

"Yeah, ten houses down."

Clem, looked in his mirror as he stopped outside the house, he could see her moving her baby finger around the bottom of her eye to remove a tear.

INDEX

europe books

Printed in the USA
CPSIA information can be obtained
at www.ICGtesting.com
LVHW091050141223
766280LV00004B/581

9 791220 139571